A Lasting Summer

A Lasting Summer

Peter Tonsoline

AuthorHouse™
1663 Liberty Drive
Bloomington, IN 47403
www.authorhouse.com
Phone: 1-800-839-8640

© 2011 by Peter Tonsoline. All rights reserved.

No part of this book may be reproduced, stored in a retrieval system, or transmitted by any means without the written permission of the author.

First published by AuthorHouse   10/25/2011

ISBN: 978-1-4634-4048-0 (sc)
ISBN: 978-1-4634-4047-3 (ebk)

Library of Congress Control Number: 2011913821

Printed in the United States of America

Any people depicted in stock imagery provided by Thinkstock are models, and such images are being used for illustrative purposes only.
Certain stock imagery © Thinkstock.

This book is printed on acid-free paper.

Because of the dynamic nature of the Internet, any web addresses or links contained in this book may have changed since publication and may no longer be valid. The views expressed in this work are solely those of the author and do not necessarily reflect the views of the publisher, and the publisher hereby disclaims any responsibility for them.

PROLOGUE

August 10, 1971

The angel of death was inbound.
An urgent announcement burst from unseen speakers.
"Medevac on the way with heavy causalities!"
Where could anyone go to escape that faceless voice? It didn't matter if you were in a surgical ward, sleeping in your hooch, or out at the perimeter wire. Those desperate words always found you.

She was sitting by herself at place no one cared to know. The supply bunker was positioned so far from the main compound that few would journey out here unless they had been ordered. But, for her it had become a sanctuary to escape the madness.

The sun simmered overhead and the air was thick with the ever-stifling humidity. Perched on a bunker roof she paid little attention to the coarse sandbags underneath. Her baggy uniform was dappled with grit and specs of shiny quartz. A tiny smile formed as she gazed at the particles of sand. Forgotten memories of a distant place and time began drifting to the surface of her mind.

Orders had been posted around the camp warning about locations to avoid. The danger of sniper fire from the jungle thicket near the perimeter was always a possibility, but it didn't matter anymore. Death lingered everywhere out there, so why try to hide.

She stared across the nearby tangles of barbed wire fencing and burned down free fire zone. In the distance a contrasting scene presented a much different picture. A farmer was tending to his crops with a water buffalo pulling a wooden plow. Heat waves shimmied off the freshly turned soil contorting the images. Children played alongside a straw hut that led into a small village. Simple dwellings formed neat rows along a dirt road with people going about their daily chores. It was such a peaceful, rural country, but it was now home to a raging monster of death and destruction.

Ten months in Vietnam had scared her forever. She had entered a world of chaos and suffering. Her hope was to bring some comfort to her duty assignment, but this heartless war had crushed her. As a trauma nurse in the 91st Evacuation Hospital in Chu Lai, she had experienced the worse possible instances of the madness that only humans could inflict on each other. Her memories carried visions of the wounded and the dying that numbed her entire being. Physically, her skin was pale and her once well-kept hair was haphazardly tied back. Her eyes sat deep into a drawn face. She weighed less now than when she was sixteen, but food was of little concern to her. She had lost her beliefs and the motives to serve here.

The chatter of approaching helicopters broke her trance. She knew where her services would be needed. Lowering her head, she fought back tears. The desire to give up and run away was overwhelming.

"All personnel report to the helipad and emergency rooms," the voice resonated through the compound.

A Lasting Summer

Whether it was her training or just routine she suddenly jumped off the bunker and ran towards the approaching storm.

The first helicopter had already landed as she approached the knoll where the casualties were being unloaded. It was never any different. Young soldiers, their bodies twisted and maimed wrapped like mummies in bloody bandages. Some remained lying on the helicopter floor. They would never again enjoy a day of life. The torn uniforms, the burnt flesh, the cries of pain, it was all there again.

A doctor was helping triage the soldiers as they were taken off the choppers. The more seriously wounded were immediately sent to surgery while those who with stable were put on stretchers along the ward entrance. The dead were unemotionally tagged, covered, and moved off the pad.

"Nurse, take over for me!" the harried doctor shouted. "This soldier needs immediate surgery and I am the only one available."

"Yes, Sir," she replied accustomed to performing this vital role as the medical helicopters brought in their damaged cargo.

A flight was arriving every two minutes. One had just left before she glanced up and saw the next one. She was amazed to see that it was still flying. Bullet holes laced the entire fuselage and most of the side plexiglass windows had been shot out. The inside was a mass of carnage. Six soldiers with all kinds of visible wounds were being dragged out as quickly as possible. The last one out was a combat medic assigned to the patrol that had been hit. His arm was mangled from a grenade and he dragged a leg in pain, but he was resisting the orderlies trying to get him onto a stretcher.

"I'm going back with this bird!" he pleaded. "My whole platoon is shot up and we have wounded still out there. Get me back! Please let me go back!"

She wasn't surprised by this medic's behavior. They rarely worried about themselves when guys from their unit were still out there. She grabbed him as he collapsed to the pad more injured than he realized. A pair of orderlies rushed over to help her.

"Please Ma'm, I need to go back," he moaned in pain and frustration. "The guys are still back there with so many wounded."

Survival in Vietnam was always the issue. Whether you were in the field or back in apparently safe areas from the action, you had to look out for yourself. She had been warned from her first day in Nam to stay out of harm's way whenever possible. Her thoughts struggled to make the sensible choice, or put herself into the maelstrom. She hesitated, but it wouldn't be a difficult decision. Somehow she always knew it would come down to this someday. She grabbed a helmet and a blood splattered flak vest from a pile of discarded equipment. The last item was the medic's field pack that she hoped still was usable.

"Let's go, guys!" She shouted above the noise of the rotating rotors and the revving engine as she leaped aboard the chopper. Her nervous fingers fumbled to get the protective vest on. The interior was covered in blood, proof of the savagery were they going. She grasped a handle next to the seat as her boots slid along the deck in the thick, red fluid that had drained from the wounded.

"Lieutenant," the pilot leaned over his seat shouting to her, "this is a very hot LZ we're going into. I don't know if we can even get back in and if we do, we'll be taking heavy fire. The NVA have the entire area surrounded."

A Lasting Summer

"I am not worried, Captain!" she fired back. "You have a job to do, and so do I."

He hesitated for a moment, but then flashed a thumb-up. Pulling back on the control stick, the helicopter twisted off the concrete pad clawing for air. As the pilot picked up speed and altitude, he banked the awkward bird towards the jungle and the awaiting tempest.

For an instant, the banking helicopter gave her a panoramic view out the open doorway. Off into the distance, she could see the deep blue, tranquil water of the South China Sea. Waves lazily rolled across a beach of gleaming white sand. It was so picturesque, hardly disturbed by the bedlam of war. For a moment, the scene caused her memories to flash back to another time, another place when things always seemed good, and life would be happy forever. A long forgotten song drifted through her mind. She smiled, but a deep sadness clutched at her heart. She knew where destiny was taking her.

CHAPTER ONE

Sunday, August 7, 2000

"Are we there yet?"

The whiny voice again. Ten miles back it was the same question. Doesn't she ever get tired of asking the same thing? In another year he would be far from all of this nonsense. He rolled down his window hoping the highway sounds would drown her out.

The scenery along the way had been steadily changing. The rolling hills lined with rows of fruits and vegetables began to merge into low-lying patches of scrub brush. The highway was leading across a narrow strip of land bordered on both sides by open water. The coastal turnpike was taking them over the man-made causeway towards the endless acres of salt marsh. The bay bridge was still about three miles away, but the rising columns of steel and cable couldn't be missed even at this distance. Birds of every type, size, and color flew out of the marshy reeds in pursuit of some avian need. The late afternoon sun was casting a soft light on the landscape.

They came from everywhere. People blocked dates, saved their money, pleaded for reservations, and counted the days when they could travel this very highway for a long awaited vacation. It was a perfect picture of the beauty of nature at one end, and a man-made playground at the other.

He stared out the window blocking out the annoyances around him. His mind wandered from boredom to frustration, but he kept thinking about things that were unanswerable. Why did this happen to him?

"Maggie," his mother spoke in a soft, motherly voice, "we will be there in about twenty minutes, honey. I know you're tired, but it won't be much longer. We're going to have such a great time at the shore that it will be worth the long drive."

Karen Freemont glanced in the rearview mirror trying to catch a glimpse of her son's expression. His eyes remained fixed, staring out the side window.

"What do you think gloomy-looking boy in the back seat?"

There wasn't any response.

"Hey, did you hear me?"

Silence.

"Drew, I am speaking to you and I expect to get a reply. Some sound that tells me you're alive!" Her tone changed from pleasant to one of annoyance. It was the usual pattern.

"Sure, whatever," he quietly responded. He didn't want to bother arguing with his mother since he was trapped in the car.

"What's wrong with you now?"

"Everything is just great," he mumbled.

"I just don't know why you're like this."

Karen Freemont responded in a rush. "Someday, something is going to make you care about things, and maybe then you will be happy."

He could sense both the frustration and sadness in his mother's voice, but it didn't matter. Maggie, his nine-year old half-sister gave her all the pleasure and joy a parent could ever hope. He just wanted to finish his senior year in high school and go away to college. Things were just different now. It wasn't the fact his mother had remarried and Maggie came into their lives. His stepfather, David, was okay. He tried to be patient and encouraging, trying to act like a father. It didn't matter. It was something that David could never understand. He knew a few kids in school who had grown up with a stepparent. He wasn't in any different situation than they were. Yet, he was. His dilemma was deeper.

Twenty minutes later, Mrs. Freemont crossed Memorial Bridge and turned the green Explorer onto Ocean Drive. The traffic was slowing down as the highway approached the outskirts of town in an assortment of vehicles. Campers trailed behind cars, RVs, trucks hauling merchandise, motorcycles, family cars and vans packed with the necessities for a vacation on the Maryland shore.

"God, the place hasn't changed much at all," his mother sighed as she peered out the side window. "Your father loved coming here so much."

"When did Daddy come here?" Maggie asked puzzled by her mother's remark.

"No, honey not your Daddy, but Drew's father back before you were born."

The light turned red causing them to stop at an intersection already filling with crossing tourists. Ocean Heights could resemble a hundred other seashore towns all along the Maryland coast. Stores selling every item appealing to the summer tourist crowd dotted Ocean Drive as it wound its way through town. A hodgepodge of screened tee shirt displays, souvenir stands, fast food joints, and beachwear stores lined the block only to be repeated on every block as far down as one could see. Flags, banners, signs and posters marked their location in every eye-catching, tourist-attracting color.

"Mom, can I please stop and buy something for Heather because I promised I would bring her back a souvenir."

"Not yet, Maggie," her mother laughed. "We haven't even settled in. I think we'll have plenty of time during the week to shop for souvenirs."

Karen turned around to catch her son's attention. "Look back, Drew, toward the end of the boardwalk. See that old looking wooden platform going out into the water. That's Captain Reader's Pier."

"It doesn't look like much," Drew replied in his usual bored tone.

"Well maybe, but your Dad told me some strange stories about the legends of that old pier."

"Are their ghosts and witches there?" asked Maggie's as her radiant blue eyes suddenly widened in apprehension.

"No, just some unusual stories and legends that people talk about," her mother said.

"Probably all made up," he added sarcastically.

"Drew, I just thought you might like to hear some things about your father."

"Sure, like I haven't already. What do you want me to say, Mom?" Drew's tone became angrier, "that these stories will bring him back?"

Before his mother could begin arguing, a horn blared from behind as the light had turned green. Mrs. Freemont drove next half-mile through town in silence as she fought back tears. Lately, every conversation with her sixteen year-old was ending up the same way. She had prayed that

A Lasting Summer

this vacation at Ocean Heights might help find the element missing in his life. At this moment she thought she had made the wrong decision.

Toward the north end of Ocean Heights, the commercial buildings were an endless mix of small motels, three-story hotels, rental cottages, bait shops, gas stations, and hot dog stands. As far as one could see, every piece of land near the beach, the boardwalk, or the ocean had some type of building or structure.

The side streets branching off the main highway transformed into established neighborhoods of a year-round beach community. These narrow roads were lined with well-kept homes with neatly arranged landscapes of flowers, bushes, and trees. Some were massive structures laced with gingerbread trim, shutters, porches, doors and colors typical of Victorian architecture. Whether it was a painted anchor, chain, lantern or mast, almost every dwelling had some type of maritime decoration.

Their SUV made a left turn on to Breakers Lane moving through a feathery arch of elm trees shading the street from the late afternoon sun. Karen pulled the Explorer into the driveway of a majestic house. A huge porch wrapped around the front with columns supporting a pitched roof. Scattered flowerboxes were overflowing with vines and flowers of every imaginable type and color. Towering over the roof of three floors was a huge turret, or Widow's Watch. Blue, violet, and pink paint outlined the entire structure.

The front screen door opened.

"Aunt Betty!" Karen called out excitedly. The elderly woman broke into a smile waving at her guests.

"Karen, dear," said the older lady as the two women embraced as they approached each other. "It's so good to see you again after all these years." Both gave into their emotions breaking into tears "I think about you and Drew every day."

"Oh, Aunt B, I so much wanted to come back here, but . . ." Karen hesitated in a hurtful pause, "I just couldn't face the memories."

"I understand," Aunt Betty gently spoke. "Sometimes it takes more than time to heal the sorrow you must feel."

Karen dabbed at her eyes forcing a smile. She felt good being here again with the woman who had been such an important part of her past. She pushed the blond strands of hair from her face allowing the warm rays of sunlight to dry her eyes.

The older woman's soothing voice helped her to regain her composure.

"Drew, Maggie," she began, "this is your Aunt Betty. The aunt I've told you so much about."

She may have been seventy-five, but the slender, gray haired woman moved with the deftness of someone twenty years younger. Maggie just about came up to her shoulders when she warmly hugged her, but Drew's six-foot frame dwarfed her. When she embraced him, she couldn't get close to getting her arms around his broad shoulders.

"My Lord, Drew, you're so tall," she began, "but mostly, I can't believe how much you look your father!"

He pulled away from her arms. His very slight smile turned dark and sour. He abruptly turned and walked toward the back of the Explorer.

"Did I say something wrong?"

Confused, Aunt Betty looked towards her niece.

Karen only shook her head and shrugged her shoulders. "Just part of being a teenager, I suppose."

"I'm glad we're here," a smiling Maggie beamed, hugging the older woman.

"So am I! Aunt Betty replied changing the subject. "I know you, your mother, and brother will have an unforgettable week here at Ocean Heights."

Drew heard his aunt's words as he pulled luggage from the back of the truck. His mood only darkened more. Confusion and loneliness crept deeper into his heart. If they only could know what he was feeling, maybe they would leave him alone.

CHAPTER TWO

"I can't believe how much they resemble each other at this age!"

Karen held the aged photo at arms length. She shaded her eyes against the setting sun, glancing back and forth between the picture and her son sitting on the wooden lawn swing. Karen was astonished at the similarity between Drew and his father back when he was sixteen.

"Andy's mother has been saying right along that even she would have trouble telling them apart right now," she continued.

"Who took Drew's picture?" Maggie asked as she peered over her mother's shoulder.

"No, honey," Aunt Betty laughed, "that's not your brother. That's his father, when he was sixteen years old."

Karen continued studying the picture of her husband posing on the very porch where they were now sitting. Tall drinks of iced tea, sweating from condensation, were perched on the table offering a refreshing break from the evening heat. After a cookout of chicken, shrimp, corn, and Aunt B's famous grilled potatoes, they moved from the patio to the wicker chairs on the porch. The older woman had dug out the old photo album from the undisturbed depths of the attic days before their arrival. She was anxious to show them more from this forgotten treasure.

"I think that was taken that last summer vacation Andy spent down here," said Aunt Betty. "I don't know what year it was, but he came down with a group of his good friends from back home. They decided to stay on their own, down in West Cove where they rented a cottage for the week."

"Wasn't that unusual?" Karen questioned. "I mean a bunch of teenage boys by themselves, not chaperoned."

"Well, perhaps by today's standards, but things and times were so much different then," Aunt Betty answered. "Oh, they still got into a bunch of trouble and some crazy predicaments, but you know, it was all harmless fun. I guess you might say part of the process of growing up."

"Andy told me so much about the good times he had down here," said Karen, "and all those stories about his friends from the neighborhood. What a collection of characters. He wasn't any better, but I think that's why I fell in love with him."

"He was such a wonderful boy." Aunt Betty's grayish eyes glistened. "I missed him so much after that summer. Oh, he kept in touch with us, but with college, and working to pay for his schooling, and then later medical school, he just never had the opportunity to spend time down here any more. Uncle Jake hoped that Andy would someday be able to come back to the shore and spend some time with us."

"He loved both of you so much, Aunt B. He always said he would like to retire here in Ocean Heights." Karen fought back tears. "It just seemed like yesterday when we planning our future with Drew, and then . . ."

"You had to move on with your life," Aunt Betty replied struggling to fight back her own tears, "and you've done a terrific job with the kids."

"I am not sure about that."

"Mom, there's nothing to do here!"

The three faces looked up in unison. Drew was standing on the porch steps with his hands thrust into the pockets of faded cut-off jeans. Along with worn sandals and a washed out tee shirt, he looked dressed for the atmosphere of the shore, but mentally he was a no show.

"I told you I would be bored," he spoke directly to his mother, "but you made me come along."

"What did you want to do, Drew, sit in your room and watch TV and play video games like you have been doing all summer long!" Karen immediately turned defensive trying to counter the verbal blows she had been receiving for the past three years. "You just need to enjoy yourself and find some things to do while we're here."

"There's nothing here but sand and bugs. I hate the sun and I don't want to walk that stupid boardwalk, or sit on the beach everyday."

"You know, Drew, there are plenty of teenagers down here your age. I bet you'll make lots of new friends like your father used to." Aunt Betty didn't realize she had put some words in her peacemaking that were going cause trouble.

"He doesn't have any friends other than Mike the Spaz," Maggie chirped up.

"Shut up twerp! I bet the sharks can't wait to chomp on you."

"Mom!"

"Drew, stop it right now!" Karen burst out in rage. "I can't stand another minute of your attitude!"

Maggie ran into the house.

Aunt Betty was on her feet. "Please, please everyone let's stop all this fussing and arguing."

"I don't want to be here!" Drew was losing control. His eyes blazed in anger, but a smoldering frustration was burning inside.

"Why did you bring me here? So I could hear about my father's life. Or maybe, hear people tell me how I look like my father and talk like him, and even act like him."

He kicked at a nearby flowerbox spilling pink and violet petunias across the wooden slats. "Don't you understand? I don't want to keep hearing about him!"

He turned and sprinted off the porch across the lawn. Karen was on her feet shouting at him and crying at the same time. Aunt Betty put her arms around her distraught niece and finally managed to bring her under some control.

"Karen, let him go. He'll be fine. He just needs to get away from us for a while."

"Aunt B, that's exactly what has been happening the past few years with him. Anytime anyone mentions his likeness to Andy, whether it is his looks or mannerisms, he instantly changes moods. If he doesn't get outright nasty and belligerent, he does exactly what you just saw. He withdraws and isolates himself."

"But Karen, he never really knew his father," Aunt Betty responded, "So, I can't understand why he would be so bitter."

"The school psychologist tried to explain it to me," Karen went on in despair. "He has no identity or connection with his father other than his resemblance, some pictures, and some obscure awards. He's struggling with the loss and the denial of ever actually having a father."

"How's David with him?"

"Oh, he's patient and tries not to be a replacement father, but Drew just won't give him a chance."

"And, Maggie?"

"She thinks the world of him, but he won't warm up to her either. He used to pick on her terribly, but as he gets older, he barely tolerates her. I know he resents me for getting married again and having another child. He only talks about graduating and going away to college, far from all of us."

Karen broke into tears. The truth and frustration poured out of her like a broken faucet. Here she was trembling and crying to a woman she hadn't seen in fifteen years. Aunt Betty, who had begged her for all these years to come and visit, now became the sounding board for her anguish. Her aunt had invited them to spend a week at the shore with her to be an enjoyable time, but things were starting off badly.

"Karen," the older woman began in a comforting tone, "I understand how difficult it has been for you. First losing Andy, trying to raise a son on your own, and then starting another family. I know you're shouldering the guilt for Drew's behavior and the missing part of his life, but he's going to be the one who has to find the meaning and direction to his life now."

"I know, but why wasn't Andy here when I needed him the most? Why did everything have to turn out this way?" Karen sobbed.

"A crystal ball is only as good as the person using it, so I imagine neither one of us will ever be able to answer those questions."

Aunt Betty led Karen up the porch steps, her arm firmly wrapped around the younger woman's waist.

"I think your decision to come here despite the painful memories will work out," she continued. "This place is just so wonderful, so healing, not only will you benefit, but perhaps Drew will find a part of his father here too."

A twinkle of hope sparkled in the older woman's eyes. She reached back into the depths of her memories and the experience of age.

"The legends say a mysterious power deep from the ocean's heart comes to shore to help someone whose soul is broken."

She hugged Aunt Betty tightly, as if that mere act could erase the pain and memories. Her words were unclear, but they brought a thread of comfort.

"Aunt Betty, if he only knew what his father was really like."

CHAPTER THREE

The dying rays of light sinking on the horizon had marked another battle lost in the sun's daily struggle with its perpetual enemy. Tendrils of blackness crept their way through the alleys transforming shadows into dark blotches as night took control. Now it was time for humans to join the conflict, as flipped switches and twisted handles illuminated the boardwalk countering the encompassing darkness. Droves of winged insects circled the lampposts attracted to the orbs of artificial sunlight.

The wooden strip was coming to life. An endless stretch of neon and artificial light blazed a trail seeping into murky cracks and crevices. In the warm night air shops left their doors open to draw in the caravan of passing tourists. Carnival games from open-sided booths challenged the wandering crowd offering an assortment of prizes from teddy bears to live goldfish. Carnies shouted from booths challenging passer-bys with their games of chance. Synthetic noise from video games and hard driving rock music blared out of speakers positioned at open doorways. Heavy, greasy fumes from deep fryers saturated the air. Overall, it was just another normal, typical night on the boardwalk.

Drew wandered through this unfamiliar environment. His impetuous sprint away from his mother and aunt had somehow brought him to the boardwalk. He couldn't remember the street name between the buildings leading

A Lasting Summer

up to the wooden structure. He wasn't even sure what street his aunt's house was on, but it didn't matter. He wasn't in any hurry to head back. His mother would probably be out walking the boardwalk later trying to find him, so he didn't care where he was.

As he casually wandered, Drew didn't notice the looks and stares from the pairs or groups of girls he passed. His athletic frame was well proportioned and muscled, hardly what might be expected of a sixteen year old. His dark tousled hair rested on a finely chiseled narrow face set with high cheekbones, prominent jaw, and eyes the color of a tropical ocean. His movie star looks went for naught, since he didn't have many friends back home, and certainly no female interests. Yet, here he was the perfect dream for any girl patrolling the boardwalk.

Strange as it seems, Drew violated every biological principle of genetics. Normal inheritance maintains an offspring will receive an equal share of traits, fifty per cent, from each parent. There is no denying this principle, but Drew was a walking violation of these laws. Regardless that his mother was truly a striking beautiful woman, the boy seemed to have inherited the full complement of traits from only one parent. He was without any doubt a perfect replication of his father.

He had seen only a few photos of his father growing up. Despite every effort to deny such a connection, he couldn't admit the truth. There was an incredible resemblance between himself and the father he never knew. This is where the problem began. He couldn't stand to hear the same remark. "Oh, you look so much like your father, or you act just like your father used to." He actually believed that his grandparents, and even his mother, would be calling him by his father's name. Too bad he even had to share the same first name. What was the big deal anyway, he often thought? To remind him of the resemblance, or make him feel like he was supposed to remember his father? He never stopped hearing the same stupid thing over and over again. The anger and frustration continued to smolder inside.

"Hey, looking for someone?"

Drew broke from his trance. The sparkling blue eyes looking directly into his, and just about at the same height, were set into a beautiful face framed with long blond hair positioned on equally long legs. She could have been the perfect model for suntan lotion or a beach volleyball player.

"Well, no, I'm not," he stuttered more out of surprise than by the captivating beauty standing in front of him. "I just sort of got here today, and well, you know, I'm trying to find my way around and . . ."

"Hey," said the girl, "I've been down here three weeks and know this strip like no one else. Come on and hook up with my friends and me. We can all hang out tonight." Three other girls stood a few feet away smiling and laughing at their friend's boldness and the boy's embarrassment. Whether their friend was just playing the boy out or whether she was serious, the other girls were very interested in him.

"What do you say, cutie?" a shorter, dark hair girl chirped up. "We got all night to cruise the boards."

Drew could feel the sweat beading on his forehead as he rushed away in embarrassment. He didn't know what to think or how to handle the situation.

"Hey guy, we don't bite!" the taller girl exclaimed, as her almost captured prey blended into the crowd.

"I think we scared him away," the shorter girl giggled. "He was really hot, but I don't think he talks to many girls."

A Lasting Summer

The rejected blond-haired girl was not one to give up so easily. "Come on, let's follow him!"

Drew dodged around people as he rushed down the boardwalk. Nervously, he kept glancing back to see if the girls were still following him. He was doing everything he could to avoid them. It wasn't that he disliked girls, or even other guys, but he found it uncomfortable to be around them because he didn't know how to act. He didn't have any real friends at school, just some kids he knew. He always seemed to say or do the wrong thing, so he kept to himself. Maybe the bitterness inside of him was somehow clouding his feelings and confidence. He wanted to be liked, maybe even by a girl. What a great feeling it would be to be part of a group and have some real friends. This is all he ever wanted, but something deep inside of him wouldn't let it happen.

Twenty minutes later he relaxed knowing he had escaped from the trailing girls. His route had taken him quite a ways down to the southern most end of the boardwalk. As he continued walking, Drew began to notice the crowd thinning out. Even the shops and food stands were lessening and more scattered from each other. The lights at this end didn't seem as bright and the paints not as vibrant. Faded advertising posters with rolled and torn edges stapled to poles heralded events that had happened years ago. He stared at the end of the boardwalk of what this area had once been. Now it was nothing more than an eyesore ready for demolition.

Drew approached an area where a chain link fence at least ten feet high stretched along the city side of the boardwalk. He could barely make out the buildings behind the fence, as they were cast in dim lights hanging from poles or absorbed in dark, gloomy shadows. Slowly walking, he gazed up at the size of the complex he thought must have been at one time some type of amusement park. Buildings with all types of decorative trim, doors everywhere, and boarded up windows filled every available wall. He figured this one large building must have been a pavilion and back behind it was an even bigger one that looked like some type of convention hall. The pavilion seemed to stretch a whole block and just when he thought he had reached the end, he was stunned to see an entire section filled with rides, game booths, a miniature golf course, food stands, a fun house and even a Ferris wheel. Almost everything he saw was in some form of disrepair and neglect. Boards and signs were randomly hanging, flopping around with the gentle offshore breeze. Windows that hadn't been boarded up were now pieces of broken glass shards. Rides were in every state of disarray, and even the miniature golf course was hardly recognizable. It was obvious this park had not been opened for years and the fence was there to prevent any trespassing.

He looked up at the faded sign in the shadows. Somehow in the poor light he thought it spelled out "Playland." Not many things impressed Drew, but he could only mumble in disbelief. "Wow, this must have been some place."

Two hundred yards past the ancient amusement park, Drew reached the end of the boardwalk. In the sparse lighting, he could see he was the only person down this far. The walkway stopped short of a sandy beach stretching into the dark water. The beach not only ran parallel to the boardwalk, but it seemed to curve around heading inland into some type of bay. On the ocean side, a huge wooden skeleton jutted out into the ebony ocean lit by a few scattered pole lights. It seemed to reach about a hundred feet out into

A Lasting Summer

the surf and was capped at the end by a covered platform forming a short T.

The boy walked off the boardwalk and stepped onto the pier. He was a little worried about its soundness, but quickly realized the old structure was pretty sturdy. The wooden planks were cracked and splintered, and smelled of fish and seawater. His senses cringed with the odor of brine and the thought of fish guts. These were even more reasons to hate this place.

Trying to remember his mother's guided tour as they drove into town, he thought there was some name for this old pier. Some guy's name, about some wharf, but he couldn't remember. He wasn't really paying much attention to his mother at the time.

Drew spotted a blue container shoved under a bench along the side railing. It looked like some type of cooler probably forgotten by a fisherman spending the day fishing off the pier. He dragged the cooler out and lifted the lid. A smile broke across his face. Submerged in melted ice water were five cans of Coors beer. It wasn't his first time with booze. He and Mike the Spaz had sneaked a few beers out of his house and had gone down to the creek to drink them. They only had two each and they had tasted pretty awful, but it was sort of a cool thing to do. It was more fun to steal the beers and not get caught drinking them than actually tasting the bitter liquid. They probably did get a little bit loaded because they spent the next half hour pushing each other into the creek. Right now, Drew was in the mood to drink the beer, lots of beer, and to let loose, to forget about this place, and . . . to forget about everything.

He plucked the cans from the cool water not wanting to take the telltale container with him. He knew he couldn't stay out on the pier drinking because a cop might be patrolling or the fisherman might return for his cooler. The beach would be okay, but his aunt had mentioned something about some beach patrol guys. The boardwalk was too open and the fence around the old amusement park was pretty high to jump. He walked down the pier with the cans of beer in his arms. He spotted a perfect location as he approached the boardwalk and looked back. Under the pier it was a maze of wooden pilings supporting the upper frame work. Waves were gently washing up the outermost pilings and there appeared to be plenty of room high up on the beach right under the pier. In the dark, and even if the moon were out, it would be next to impossible to see him sitting under the low part of the pier drinking the cans of beer.

An hour or two might have gone by. He couldn't really tell or even cared, but three empty beer cans were lying in the sand, and he was holding a half finished fourth. He stared out toward the ocean. A soft light from a rising moon reflected from the crests of breaking waves. The sound of the incoming tide increased in volume and duration. His mind was racing with a myriad of mixed feelings and thoughts. The alcohol was tearing down barriers, releasing a flood of emotions he had never experienced before. He was losing control and feeling overwhelmed by things that he couldn't explain.

Things were about to change for him. He was so close to graduating from high school, leaving his mother, and starting his own life, yet he wasn't ready. That deep void in his existence kept blocking everything he wanted to do.

"It wasn't fair," he thought. "It just wasn't fair what had happened to him."

Drew's vision wasn't blurred enough to see the gossamer cloud of mist forming out over the ocean. It seemed strange for this fog-like cloud to suddenly appear out of nowhere. He remembered from his science class that fog could form with differences in temperature between the air and open water. It was kind of neat watching the shifting, iridescent mist drift closer toward the beach enveloping everything within its swirling folds. In a few minutes, the spectral cloud had obscured everything in front of him except for a few wooden pilings.

Drew was getting nervous. He forced his eyes to focus straight ahead into a narrow corridor forming in the thickly layered mist. The alcohol had numbed his senses and his thinking, but he was sober enough to know something was wrong.

Suddenly, an outline of a figure began to take shape. Drew squinted trying to pierce the drifting strands of vapor. The image began to materialize. Strangely enough it resembled a fisherman.

The man was wearing high rubber boots and black oil slicker typical of the commercial fishermen who worked the coastal waters. A faded mustard color, old-fashioned life jacket was wrapped across his chest and midsection. Even though it was a calm night with the exception of the sudden fog bank, the person had the hood from his jacket drawn so far over his head that his face was covered by a shadow.

"Howdy," echoed a gravely voice from deep within the hood. It sounded like a man's voice despite the fact the boy had not yet seen a face.

"Hi," Drew replied. "You've been out fishing?"

"Sort of in a way," said the faceless form silhouetted by a shroud of mist. "I came in with the tide and the fog."

"Yeah, that's cool." The boy slurred his words. "Not a good night to be out on the ocean."

"Any night is a good one, if you're out at sea and the wind and waves are calm," the voice remarked.

"Catch any fish?"

"No, but I was out for other things."

"Oh," Drew returned in a confused way, "sure thing."

"See you've been tipping a few. Have an extra one?"

"Sure, you can have the last one," said Drew nervously.

He pulled the remaining beer from the sand and extended it towards the figure. A hand, leathery and bronzed from the sun, and skin wrinkled with age reached out from the sleeve of the jacket. At least the figure was human and not an apparition. The boy breathed in relief.

The calloused fingers ripped the tab off the can and as he tilted his head back to pour the liquid into his mouth, the hood slipped back, finally revealing the features of his drinking companion. Hard stubble covered a grizzly face crisscrossed with cracks and furrows. His hair was long and wind blown mixed with brown and gray patches. Bushy, thick eyebrows sat along eyes the color of steel and looked just as hard. Despite the bulky clothing, it was evident the man had a thick, powerful frame toughened by years at sea. He projected an imposing stature and there certainly was nothing soft to this man.

"Have a fight with a girl," the old man said, not really interested in an answer, "or you just thought you'd like to tie one on tonight."

"Not really." Drew stared ahead, but started to feel the anger rise. "Why would you care?"

"Temperamental are we like some flowery cabin boy."

"Yeah, sure, whatever you say."

"It's not very often I wander into someone sitting by themselves under this old pier, especially trying to drink their troubles away."

Drew hesitated. He wasn't sure were this conversation was heading.

"I guess I just needed a place to think things out," he slowly responded. Drew took a long drink from the beer left in his can. "I wasn't planning on meeting anyone out here."

"Suppose you have a point." This time the old man seemed a bit concerned. "Your parents know you're down here?"

"No, and who cares," Drew replied abruptly. "My mother is always worrying about me and never leaves me alone."

"What about your father?"

Drew remained silent.

"Something wrong?" the fisherman asked.

"I don't have a father."

The old man picked his words carefully. "Is your father living somewhere else?"

"I wish it were that simple," Drew mumbled frustrated words. "At least then I would know who he was."

"What do you mean? Where is he?"

The words were always hard for Drew to say. "He's dead."

"Sorry about that," said the grizzled figure in a sympathetic tone. "It's a tough thing to lose a parent when you're growing up. I suppose the best thing you can do now is remember him."

The alcohol was causing him to say more about how he felt than he ever had, and to a perfect stranger. "I can't remember anything because I never knew him. I wasn't even two years old when he was killed."

Drew paused deep in thought. His words were slurred with beer and emotion. "He was a doctor. On the way home from the hospital one night, he stopped to help some people in a car accident. A tractor trailer never saw the accident and crashed into the car killing him."

He put his hands over his eyes. "He didn't have to stop and help. He didn't have to get killed and leave me and my mother alone."

"He was doing what his life was about," the fisherman offered. "He was a doctor and he was helping someone who needed him."

"The hell he did!" Drew exploded. "He needed to live his own life and be there for us. We're the only ones who needed him!"

"So why are you angry? Because your father died or he wasn't there for you?"

"Both! I hate it because I never knew him! I don't know anything about him. What he liked, what he did growing up, who his friends were, what he thought about . . ."

Drew fought back the tears. "I am only left with the same old line 'You look so much like your father and you act so much like him.' I can't stand to hear it anymore!"

"Mister, why did it have to happen this way? I never even had the chance to know him."

The old man took a final swig from his beer and crushed the can tossing the crumpled aluminum into the sand.

"Drew, sometimes life is not always the way you want it to be," said the nameless man in a soft, understanding voice. "Your father didn't pick his time to die and leave you and your mother behind."

The boy jumped to his feet in astonishment.

"How do you know my name? What do you know about me?"

A Lasting Summer

The old fisherman pulled the hood over his head. He began to fade into the enveloping mist, his form vanishing like a shimmering mirage.

"Who are you?" Drew shouted.

A voice drifted out from the fog.

"Your time has come to learn, Drew. Begin by seeking the knowledge of the Flower."

Drew turned to run from the fading image and the terrifying acknowledgement. His feet broke into a sprint, but he only managed to take three steps before a blinding pain struck him across the head. His legs weakened and he crumpled to the soft comfort of the sand. Barely lifting his head, the last thing he saw was the old fisherman silhouetted in the twisting spirals of mist. Then, a thick blackness absorbed him.

CHAPTER FOUR

Monday, August 8

A sunrise along the ocean is never the same as the day before. Strands of light reached over the eastern horizon as usual, but the colors of the sky and water play an unpredictable game of mixing and matching, clashing or coordinating to whatever seemed to be their moods for the day. This morning's artist was whipping up a tapestry of azure pinks and blues draped against an imperial blue ocean. It was spectacular, if you were up at dawn, but more so, if your eyes were open.

A prone figure was lying in the dank, gloomy darkness of the overhead pier. He could have remained lying there for quite some time, if it weren't for the cold water of the incoming tide rushing up to his toes. The strange sensation on his bare feet didn't jolt him awake, but it at least made him open his eyes. He was vaguely aware of a light, yet it didn't appear to be a night-light and this certainly wasn't his bed.

Drew sprang up to a sitting position. The sun was straight ahead showing about a quarter of itself at the edge of the horizon. The incoming tide was rolling in a smooth, calm sea and nudging at his bare toes. The spectacular sunrise had little effect on the dull, throbbing pain in his

A Lasting Summer

head. He reached up and felt a lump bulging from his forehead.

"What the hell," he moaned. Things were slowly drifting back. "All that beer I drank. I wonder if this is what a hangover feels like."

His head was pounding and spinning simultaneously, yet his scrambled memory started to piece together some coherent thoughts.

"That guy, that old fisherman," he groaned, "he must have bashed me across the head with something." Still dazed, he looked up and saw a low overhanging crossbeam bracing the bottom of the pier. It was becoming clear to him now that he never saw what hit him because he had run headfirst into it in the darkness. The thought that he wasn't attacked by the strange man didn't lessen the major headache crashing around somewhere between his ears. He staggered to his feet grabbing at the beam trying to maintain his balance in the loose sand underfoot and a spinning equilibrium.

Staggering through the sand, he finally gained the solid reaches of the boardwalk. His throbbing head wasn't feeling any better, but he was beginning to gain some stability. Drew looked down the long stretch of wooden planks trying to get his bearings. The sun was now perched above the horizon, so he thought it must be around sunrise whatever time that was. Oddly enough, it didn't seem like there were any people around. There always seemed to be some nuts out jogging or walking this early in the morning and the boardwalk seemed like a perfect place. Yet, it appeared deserted. He hadn't walked more than hundred yards when his spinning eyes almost rotated out of their sockets.

"What the hell is going on?" Drew blurted out in astonishment.

There was no one around to answer the boy's sudden outburst. Even if there had been someone there, one would have taken Drew for some wacky teenager probably out partying late last night. However, there wasn't a thing out of the ordinary on this beautiful summer morning on the Maryland shore.

Drew felt the beer well up in the pit of his stomach. Waves of nausea crashed into his already teetering brain. He stood at the edge of the same boarded, broken down abandoned amusement park he had passed the night before, except now it was different. Beautiful bright reds, yellows, blues, greens, every imaginable color adorned ornate, perfectly kept and maintained buildings. The debris and rubble were gone. Windows were covered with sheets of solid glass. Unbroken light bulbs hung on every pole. Banners and flags, colorful and new waved in the gentle offshore breeze. Legible signs across food and game stands advertised their carnival delicacies or winnable prizes. Rides were propped open and positioned waiting for the day's riders. The pavilion, the miniature golf course and even the Ferris wheel were all there. Yet, the imposing fence separating the park from the boardwalk, keeping the curious away, was gone with the suggestion it had never been there to begin.

The sign proclaiming "Playland" gleamed in the early morning sun as Drew leaned over the rail of the boardwalk puking his guts out. It probably was the beer he drank the night before or something he had eaten at Aunt Betty's he kept telling himself, as the last of his stomach contents emptied. Still bent over the railing, he slowly twisted his head around to see if the illusion disappeared. Playland remained bright and shiny and big as life as he went back to puking, but now in dry heaves.

A Lasting Summer

Collapsing to the wooden deck, he sat with his back toward the railing and the ocean. He remained in a fixed position staring at the sight before him. Drew could only figure that somehow in the dark of night and maybe the mood he was in, he had mistakenly pictured the amusement park looking abandoned and ready for the wrecking ball. Yet somehow, he knew there had been a fence, a high chain link fence because he had felt it with his own hands . . .

"Hey, you commie piss-ant!"

He turned toward the voice. Two boys about his age were walking toward him.

"What the hell! You look like dog-crap warmed over." This unflattering announcement came from the other boy.

Drew glanced up at the two figures. He had no idea who they were or what they were talking about, yet for some reason it seemed as if they knew him.

"We've been searching the boardwalk since six," the redhead said, "and how the hell did you ever end up here?"

"God, you even smell like crap," said the other boy who had first spotted him. He was wiry looking, skinny with long arms and legs, his narrow face topped with dark short, curly hair. Black framed glasses sat on a pointy nose. He took the cigarette he was smoking and flicked it over the railing. "I figured that little blonde eyeing you up took you home with her, and she must have because you not even wearing the same clothes you had on last night."

"Andy, what happened to your head?" asked the redhead as he knelt next to the sitting figure.

"I ran into a beam under the pier trying to get away from," Drew responded touching the lump on forehead. "There was this guy, and he started telling me . . ." Suddenly panic and terror overwhelmed him. Within a night's span, another two totally complete strangers knew his name in an area that he had never been to before in his life.

"I told you, Red he was hooked up with some shore chick."

"Who are you guys?" Drew sat motionless, unable to move and completely bewildered.

"Andy, it's me Pat, Red O'Donnell. What the hell is wrong with you? You look like you don't know us."

Drew stared at him.

"Red, I think maybe he has a concussion or something from the size of that goose-egg on his head. Maybe he has amnesia." The other boy looked concerned.

"You're right, Roach, he's really out of it. We need to get him checked out. I thought I saw a first-aid station down near Packer's hamburger stand. Let's take him there right now."

The two strangers grabbed Drew under each arm forcing him to his feet. Dizziness was clouding his brain and he still felt nauseous, but regardless, he knew something was terribly wrong.

"Hey," Drew mumbled trying to suppress his panic, "can I borrow someone's cell phone to call my mom?"

The boys stopped momentarily walking him down the boardwalk. "Andy, your mom is back in Columbus," Red said. "We're here with the boys, on our own. Don't you remember?"

A blank look covered Drew's face.

"You commie bastard," Roach chirped up mixed with a nervous laugh, "you really are screwed up. Nothing a few brews can't fix. Hey by the way, what the hell is a cell phone?"

"You guys are lying. My mother was at Aunt Betty's house last night. We just got in yesterday."

"Good start. You remembered arriving here yesterday," said Red, "and we did stop in and see your Aunt Betty, but your mother is back home."

"I need to get to my Aunt's house right away."

"That's what got us into trouble," Red continued. "Your Aunt thought you were with us last night and we thought you slept at her house. She stopped in early to say goodbye and you came up missing."

"Don't worry, we covered your ass," Roach added as he pulled out a pack of cigarettes and lit one up. "We told her you were fishing or something along the beach. We weren't going to tell her you were out with some harlot you know!"

"She was in a hurry to leave and your uncle was out in the car waiting."

"My uncle," Drew gasped, "is dead!"

"Yeah, sure." Red began leading the stunned boy down the boardwalk. "He looked pretty alive yesterday afternoon when we were all talking about football and the AFL. He loves Broadway Joe Namath and hopes he gets a chance to play those candy asses in the NFL someday."

"Where were they going?" Drew struggled with believing what he had just heard. "I need to talk to my aunt right now to figure out what's going on."

"Andy, they left early this morning to visit your grandmother in Phoenix. They won't be back for two weeks."

More confused than before, Drew said nothing more as the two boys walked with him. They continued with some idle chatter, but the words were lost on him. Yet, he began to notice a change along the way. This lower part of the boardwalk, the section that appeared so old and run down last night, seemed revitalized. He was seeing a transformation to the surroundings he had witnessed at the amusement park. The whole area was lined with new-looking shops and concession stands. Also, a few more people were out and about along the boardwalk. Glancing at them, nothing seemed out of the ordinary at first, but now he noticed something was different. Their clothes looked like casual wear for the beach, yet they were ancient, more like old-fashioned things he remembered seeing in some videos from his American history class. Even their hair was strange, cut and styled in some weird way. He could barley breath. Something was wrong with what he was seeing.

Ten minutes later, the boys had arrived at a one-story, cement block building just off the boardwalk next to the beach. He remained silent during their walk, but was picking up on some things from their conversation. They were part of a group of friends all from the same neighborhood. They had just arrived at Ocean Heights for a week of summer vacation without any parents or supervision. Somehow he was a member of this group, or they thought.

"Now don't go telling these guys you were drinking last night, you perverted hippie," said Roach with his usual banter. "They'll bust your ass for drinking underage and hooking up with one of their local chicks."

Three college age guys were sitting around a large table behind a counter covered with report sheets and clipboards. A news report was coming out of a radio perched off on a side windowsill. The people in the office were super tan and had bleached blond hair combed back in long waves, but not hanging past their neck. They had tee shirts pulled over long baggy swimming suits and they appeared to be lifeguards ready to start their shift.

"Help you guys?" one asked as he looked up from a stack of papers.

A Lasting Summer

Red took charge. "Yeah, our friend was out surfing early this morning and when he wiped out, the board kicked back and hit him across the head. He might have blacked out, we're not sure, but we're kind of worried because he can't seem to remember very much about anything."

"Captain," another member of the office group called around a corner toward a smaller hidden office, "would you mind checking this out?"

A slightly older man emerged from the office. He appeared in almost the same attire, but looked more distinguished and in charge. Being tan and in great shape couldn't conceal the ugly twisted scar down the side of one leg and the slight limp to his walk.

"What's wrong guys?" he asked.

Red retold the incident. When he finished, he made his request. "We were told that you might be able to provide some first aid for our friend. See, we just arrived and we don't want to take him to a hospital and then have him call his parents back home."

The older man scrutinized the situation. "Pretty nasty lump for a surfboard to make," he began.

Drew just nodded as the man began to exam his eyes and the bump on his head. He had a million questions, but how do you ask anything, if you don't know what's going on. The best thing at the moment, Drew figured, was to keep quiet and somehow get in touch with his mother.

"It seems like you ran into the board at full speed."

The three boys held their breaths.

"Funny thing, but I thought you get wet when you surf," the Captain continued, "and I didn't know they served beer on board."

Red rolled his eyes. In their rush to get Drew some help, they hadn't thought out their story.

"I think it might be more useful if you guys were just honest with me."

"Sorry about that, sir," Red said in a quiet voice, "we didn't want to get our friend in trouble." He went on to add as much detail as he knew.

"I know a little more now and can appreciate your concern for your friend."

For the next few minutes, the Captain gave Drew a thorough examination, asking him a number of questions which he had trouble answering.

"Well, Andy, you have a mild concussion that will probably give you a nasty headache for a few days. The amnesia is common and should clear up if you take it easy and stay away from the beer."

"Oh, don't you worry," said Roach, "we'll dry out this alcoholic, drunk redneck for the rest of this week."

The Captain smiled and suggested Drew use the rest room to clean himself up. When he had left, the older man offered some advice to the two remaining boys.

"Guys, your friend has a pretty good bump on his head, nothing serious, but the amnesia part is pretty severe. You never know with a head injury the extent of some brain malfunction, and in the case of your friend it's probably a temporary loss of memory. You don't have to worry because he'll be back to normal in a few days, but in the meantime, just be patient with him and understand his dilemma."

"Is there anything we should be doing for him?" asked Red.

"Yes, it would help if you mention everything you know about him, your friends, school, girls, sports, cars, and you know, things that guys your age like to talk about. All these will start to make sense to him after awhile and help him get his memory back that much sooner."

A Lasting Summer

The boys again thanked the Captain for his help as he was leaving the building to begin his morning rounds along the beach lifeguard stations. By then, Drew had returned.

"Hey he's a pretty cool guy," Red mentioned to one of the younger lifeguards. "He really looked like he knew what he was doing. What's he a doctor or something?"

"Yeah, he's cool. He knows how to take care of any injury because he's been through the worse."

"What do you mean?"

The lifeguard paused for a moment. "He doesn't talk about it, but we found out he was an Army medic. Last year, he was in Vietnam in a place called the Ia Drang Valley. Apparently his entire unit was blown to shit and he was wounded so badly he was discharged."

"Gook bastards!" Roach jumped in the conversation. "I can't wait to join the Marines and get over to Nam and blow away some of those little, yellow dinks."

Drew was overwhelmed. This entire past hour had been a blur of confusion mixed with a pounding headache. He kept telling himself it was all some wild dream, he was going to wake up, and his mother would be standing there. He just wanted all this to go away, so he remained silent not giving into this out of control nightmare.

"Surf's up Ocean Heights!" blared out of the radio.

Drew focused his attention on the DJ's voice.

"It's seven-thirty on your fifty-five AM dial, and this is the sand-man, the class-man, Jack The Mack Knife pounding out those tunes all morning for your sun-soaking pleasure. Let's start the half-hour with those dudes from California, the Beach Boys and "Little Surfer Girl."

That oldies music again, Drew thought. Is this the only kind of music the play around here? He concentrated hard forcing himself not to get caught up any deeper in his nightmare. These two guys were acting like they were his long-time, best friends, and treating him like he was here. Maybe his head injury was causing him to hallucinate. His eyes wandered around the room. Suddenly, the blood washed from his face and his stomach twisted in spasms. A cold stream of sweat ran down the middle of his back.

"Oh my God," he moaned in frozen terror. His eyes never left the calendar with the picturesque beach scene, the days of August, and the large printed year . . . 1965.

CHAPTER FIVE

The morning sun was gaining height, changing the color of the ocean water stretched below to a deeper, richer blue. Clusters of gulls and other sea birds glided on the gentle incoming breeze. The boardwalk was also starting to come to life as workers opened stands and dragged out display racks for the anticipated morning shoppers. With the cloudless sky and rising temperature, it was shaping up to be another perfect summer day on the shore.

The three boys left the lifeguard station and were walking in the opposite direction they had come from. Red shuffled along as the skinny Roach lit a cigarette and bantered about his past experiences along the Maryland coast. Apparently, he had lived in that area for quite a few years and had spent many summers along the shore with his family. Red was captivated by the many stories his skinny, animated partner never seemed to get tired of telling.

"This is just so cool to be here," mentioned Red. "I can't believe we talked our parents into this. What do you think, Andy?"

No reply came from their friend with the lump on his forehead and a thousand questions spinning around in his head. Drew was still numb from what he had seen at the lifeguard station.

"There was no way this could be 1965," he kept thinking. Going back into the past was the plot for movies and books, but this never could happen in real life. It just was some mix up, or maybe a joke his mother was playing on him. He would get this mess straightened out soon enough and find the explanation for this whole charade. Still, why were these two guys even bothering to stay with him?

The rows of stores lining the boardwalk grew fewer in number and soon began to give way to an odd assortment of beach houses. They seemed to come in all size and shapes, as beautiful restored Victorian three and four story buildings merged into rows of inexpensive, poorly maintained cottages. North Cove was the tourist attraction for weekly rentals, so their rapid turnover didn't allow the repair and desperately needed face lifting. Despite their condition, there wasn't a cottage for rent in North Cove.

The boys headed toward a one-story cottage set back a few streets from the boardwalk. They had left the solid wooden walkway and now found themselves trudging through sand or following a cracked asphalt road separating the rows of beach cottages. Two more boys sat on a narrow porch in front of the one-floor, aqua blue house they approached.

"Hey, nice work, you guys did find him," said Jeff Hickson. Both boys were around the same age as the rest, but here one was appreciably taller. Jeff Hickson was medium height with wavy dark hair and sleepy, pale-gray eyes. He held a bottle of Pepsi in one hand and some type of breakfast food in the other. The other boy, John Reeger, was six-foot three, slender, but not skinny like Roach. His good-looking features were covered by long blondish-brown hair styled differently from the other boys. He was sitting on the porch railing, but did not offer any conversation.

A Lasting Summer

"You were right," Red began, "we found him under the boardwalk up near the old pier. The only problem is he doesn't remember anything.

Pat O'Donnell and Roach told their friends what had happened. The boys were laughing at the situation their one friend had already gotten into, and they hadn't even been there a day. Drew remained quiet and withdrawn, not only because of his confusion, but also from the throbbing in his head.

"Where are Skip and Howie?" Red questioned.

"Howitt is still sleeping, of course," Jeff answered, "and Skip took off by himself."

"I told you guys not to bring him along," said Roach annoyed at the mention of Skip's name. "He acts weird most of the time, or just plain moody."

"We've known him longer than we've known you," John Reeger spoke up, "and he might be strange, but he's still our friend."

"Sure, Reegs, I know you guys stick together."

Drew stood back absorbing the conversation. It was becoming clear that these boys had known each other for a long time and that Roach was apparently a new comer. Great, he thought, a bunch of friends together at the beach, but who really cares. Yet, for some strange, stupid reason they seemed to be accepting him as someone they knew. From the very first contact with the two boys, they had treated him as if he was just one of their friends. Something was incredibly wrong.

"So, Andy, what was that chick's name from last night?" Jeff snickered with the thought that meeting girls at the shore was as easy as Roach said it would be.

"There wasn't a girl, and my name is Drew."

"You John Birch, right-wing, hippie freak," Roach bellowed as his eyes widened almost beyond the dark rims of his glasses. "You get smacked in the head and now you want to be called Drew instead of Andy. What are you some queer from Greenwich Village?"

This good-natured attack brought plenty of laughter from the other guys. Drew, on the other hand, decided the less he said might be the best thing right now. Red seemed to be the more sympathetic member of the group, so maybe he could persuade him to take him to his Aunt's house.

"What the hell are you idiots laughing at? Can't a guy get any sleep around here?"

Howie Gillman, better known as Howitt, had strolled out on the porch. He was quite different looking from the other members of the group. He was short, overweight, and non-athletic looking. His round, baby-face was topped with tight, wiry, curly reddish-brown hair everyone accused him of bleaching. A cigarette rested between his fingers and he always dressed for the occasion. Today, it was cut-off jeans, no shoes, no shirt and rolls of fat hanging over the place where there might have been a belt.

Drew followed the boys inside. There were duffle bags of clothes scattered everywhere and the adjoining bedrooms were in similar disarray. The kitchen table was covered with every imaginable type of cereal, doughnuts, cookies, milk, orange juice, soda and anything else that sounded edible to a group of sixteen-year old boys. Breakfast was unplanned and a basic free for all. It was fairly obvious that this, and other meals, would be the same way for their entire stay.

An hour later, most of the boys had wandered off toward the boardwalk, while a couple decided a few extra hours of sleep would be a better choice. Drew managed to corner

Red alone and was trying to convince him to help him find his aunt's house.

"I know you think I am crazy," Drew began, "but I need to get to my aunt's house, so I can find out what is going on around here."

Red thought it was a waste of time, since Drew's aunt and uncle had already left, but he was concerned about his friend's amnesia. Maybe this would help him to remember.

"Listen, Andy, if you think it will make you feel better, I'll take you there, said Red, "but promise me you won't tell the guys."

Drew agreed knowing that everything would work out.

The two boys had walked about six blocks from their cottage. Drew remembered seeing so many of these homes the day before when his mother drove down the same streets. He spotted his aunt's house and his heart started to race. Finally, he thought, this confusion could be cleared up and he would learn what the heck was going on. His mother's Explorer wasn't in the driveway, but maybe she was out looking for him. He sprinted up the steps desperately pulling on a locked doorknob and knocking at the same time.

"Aunt Betty, please open up. It's me Drew!"

His plea went unanswered. Sure enough, the house appeared to be closed up and locked for an extended absence by the owners.

"Maggie, if you're in there, let me in!"

A deadly silence was his only reply. Panic began to tear away again at his composure.

"Andy, I told you she wouldn't be here." Red tried to calm his partner's desperation. "Come on, let's head back to the house. Maybe a shower and some rest will make you feel better."

"Where is everyone?" Drew bellowed, kicking at the closed door and actually splintering a portion of the lower frame. Red grabbed Drew's arm pulling him away the door.

"Andy, calm down would you! I wasn't lying about your aunt being gone, but I thought you had to see for yourself."

Drew yanked his arm free of Red's grasp. He wanted to holler out in anger, but remained silent trying to shake off the overwhelming feelings of panic and disappointment. Everything was just so wrong.

Red led the way back to the boardwalk, entering from another side street leading up to the makeshift sidewalk. He talked all the way, telling Drew they were close friends since elementary school, and now they were both going into their senior year at Bishop Simmons High School. Drew nodded pretending his recollection at things he knew nothing about, yet he vaguely remembered his mother telling him that his father had graduated from Bishop Simmons. However, it seemed anything relating to his father was always changing. Bishop Simmons High School situated in the city proper of Columbus had closed down ten years ago.

"Hey, Andy, let's stop for a milkshake." Red motioned toward Smythe's Ice Cream Station. A giant shape of a cone perched on the roof in full view of any potential customers looking down the length of the boardwalk.

"No, screw the shake," Drew blurted out. "Go in yourself and leave me alone."

Pat O'Donnell didn't acknowledge the hostile attitude. Once he disappeared into the ice cream shop, Drew raced down the boardwalk desperately searching for a pay phone.

A Lasting Summer

He fumbled for a quarter in the pockets of his shorts. His hand was shaking as he aimed the quarter at the pay slot of the phone. To his surprise, the call was only a dime and not the usual twenty-five cents. A quick search produced the money needed to end this nightmare. He began with his mother's cell phone number that quickly responded with the mechanical voice of "no such number." Next, he added the necessary amount and dialed home to Columbus. An older, scratchy female voice answered quite annoyed at Drew's insistence that this was his home phone number. The voice agreed he was dialing the correct number, but there was no Freemont family living there. Panic again began to overwhelm him. He remembered David's phone number at his printing business and quickly dialed that up. His hope plummeted as the phone message retuned "no such number."

He slumped on the boardwalk. This seemed to be a story from that old show 'The Twilight Zone', or maybe a Stephen King novel. It just couldn't be happening to him. Here he was with a bunch of strangers, vacationing on the Maryland shore, cut off from his family, thirty-five years earlier than when it was yesterday, and not sure of what to do next.

"Let's cruise." Red's voice broke Drew's thoughts.

"Something is really wrong," Drew muttered. "There's no way I should be right here right now."

"What do you mean by that? We've been planning this trip for a year mostly because you came here before to stay with your aunt."

"No, you don't understand what I'm talking about. I'm not who you think I am."

Red tossed his empty container into a nearby barrel. His eyes bunched up behind the frame of his glasses. "Yeah,

Andy, you're damn right. You're acting like some jerk-off with a huge attitude. I've known you just about my whole life, but I don't know who you are right now. I hope you're acting this way because you're a little messed up. If there is something bothering you about us, you can head back home right now."

Drew didn't respond. Red had appeared the friendliest of the group, but now he seemed to be pissed off. Typical, Drew thought, everyone acted that way around him sooner or later. He was a loner, a person who never seemed to attract kids his own age to do things with or just hang out. His mother always blamed his moodiness and his negative attitude towards people, so no one wanted to be around him very long. Consequently, his defenses started to rise, as the doubt of believing and trusting in others could actually be possible. When it really mattered, no one cared, so why should it be any different now, wherever he was.

"Yeah, ok, if you say so." Drew backed off.

Red shook his head in bewilderment. He had known Andy almost his entire life. Now, suddenly, he was acting like some arrogant jerk, like a person he didn't even know anymore. Maybe the blow to his head was causing this sudden change in Andy's personality, but it was pushing him to his limits right about now.

The walk back to the cottage remained silent. Drew didn't want a confrontation and certainly didn't want to hear about things he knew nothing about. He did remember from biology class that people with head injuries, strokes or senility would sometimes have bouts of amnesia, but that wasn't explaining any of this. Yet, he did recall his teacher talking about genetic residue in offspring. Somehow, not only were physical traits passed onto children in genes, pieces of memory could also be sent through the genetic

A Lasting Summer

mechanism of inheritance. Yeah, he looked like his father, but could he have acquired some of his memory from his dad's chromosomes? Maybe he was lying somewhere in a coma, experiencing all of this in a hallucinatory state. Drew was inherently quite intelligent, but this was too much for him to understand.

The boys reached their cottage and found the rest of the group had left for the beach. It was late morning, but the sun's rays were burning down through a cloudless sky, with the temperature climbing past the eighty-degree mark.

"Too damn hot to hang around here," Red mentioned. "I am going to the beach with the rest of the guys. If you want to take a shower, your bag is in that far bedroom with my stuff and Roach's."

Drew nodded his, but was preoccupied with his thoughts.

"You might want to shower and change your clothes. We probably will spend the whole afternoon down there, so you can sleep on the beach."

Red was already moving out the screened door leaving Drew standing alone in the cottage. He worked his way toward the far bedroom peering into each of the other rooms. Typical of most teenagers, clothes were scattered, spread and thrown around in an unrecognizable disarray of types and colors. His apparent room was a bit more organized and he saw an unmade cot with a large zippered gym bag placed on top. Only one bag remained unopened and he wondered to whom it might belong. He pulled the zipper to open the bag and started to remove a stack of neatly folded tee shirts, shorts, toiletries and an assortment of miscellaneous items. Tucked into one corner, he found a paperback book with a paper folded inside of it. When he took the book out, he was surprised at the title. John Steinbeck's, *The Grapes of Wrath,* was hardly what he expected to find. Strange, he thought, he had just read this in English class at school and actually enjoyed it more than he had expected. But why was this in this boy's bag? The folded paper seemed to be acting as a bookmark and there was typing on one side of it. The top was in letterhead form and read "Bishop Simmons High School" and the next lines described a summer reading list. At the very beginning was Steinbeck's novel along with a list of five more with an explanation of what would be required from the readings.

Drew scanned to the bottom of the page and abruptly collapsed to the floor clutching the paper in his hand. The bad nightmare had just gotten worse.

"Oh, my God, oh my God . . ." he just kept repeating over and over. His eyes were locked in a fixed stare of disbelief and confusion. At the bottom of the paper, he read the neatly printed name Andy Michaels, dated June 17, 1965. Andy Michaels was his deceased father's name.

He couldn't remember how long he sat on the floor struggling to regain his composure and his sanity. Ever since he had woken up from his collision with the pier beam, things just kept getting stranger, and freakier. What was this all about? People who knew you by name, guys who just came along and made you part of their group, calendar dates going back to 1965, and now this, a piece of paper with his father's name unmistakably written across the bottom.

There had to be an explanation somewhere, but where or whom could he turn to for some answers? So far, none of these people looked even vaguely familiar, plus they all dressed like freaks from some old movie. Well, he still felt like a real person no matter whether he was somewhere in the Twilight Zone, and a shower would probably help him to settle down. Drew grabbed a dry towel, a toiletry

A Lasting Summer

kit, shorts and shirt from the gym bag. The clothing was pretty old-fashioned, but they were clean and seemed to be just about his size. The person who owned this stuff didn't appear to be around, so what the heck.

Twenty minutes later, he walked from the bedroom into the kitchen. Earlier that morning he couldn't have looked at any food, but hunger pangs were gnawing in his stomach right now. The assortment of cereals and snack food littering the table were endless, but he settled for a bowl of Cheerios and milk that appeared to be fresh. He sat outside on the porch running the length of the cottage. His mind still was wrapped in his dilemma, but he began to take in the scene around him. The whole area was a hodgepodge of cottages, bungalows and garage-like dwellings covered with an array of beach chairs, towels, blankets and just about anything that a person could float on.

Drew cursed in disgust thinking this whole mess could have been avoided if he just would have stayed home and not been forced to come on this stupid trip with his mother and sister. His mind raced ahead trying to figure out what he would do.

The early afternoon sun was pushing the temperature to an uncomfortable level keeping Drew outside. The small cottage didn't allow for much circulation and the low ceilings were causing the air to stifle. For the heck of it, Drew decided to walk down to the beach. If any reason, his interest was piqued to find out more about this odd assortment of boys. Strangely, they all seemed to know him. Maybe one of them could give him some clue how his father's name was written on that slip of paper.

A short walk later he was standing on the boardwalk looking down on the beach. The beach was jammed with every size and shape of bodies making it impossible to tell where one group ended and the next began. He never could understand the attraction to the sun, beach, and ocean, but this was proof that people must somehow enjoy it. The glaring sun made his eyes water, so he had trouble finding the boys from the cottage.

It probably was all in his imagination. Drew began to reason through the situation and was finding some reassurance. "These guys are nothing more than part of my dream," he thought.

"Hey, Andy, we thought you were back at the house."

He turned around. His hopes quickly dimmed as the three boys were approaching him. They were from the cottage and he couldn't remember their names, and he wasn't imagining them.

"Jeff," said the medium height boy sensing some problem. "And, this is Reegs, and Howitt."

Drew remained motionless and unresponsive.

"You really are screwed up!" the short, fat Howie Gillman sarcastically blurted out. "He acts like he doesn't even know us. I told you we should have sent him home this morning."

"Cram it, Howie!" the taller John Reeger spoke out. "We send him home like this and we're all up the creek."

"Shut up!" said Jeff irritated at the comment. "Look, it's only been a few hours since we got him back here, and Red did say that it might be a few days before anything makes sense to him. So why don't we just stop pissing about the whole mess."

No one argued. The situation seemed to be settled, at least for now.

Jeff grabbed Drew's arm leading the way. The boys were weaving and twisting through the endless rows of prone bodies stretched across the sand. The smell of suntan lotion tinted the breeze coming in from the ocean, and a countless mix of musical sounds danced through the air. The sights distracted Drew. Every type of girl covered the sandy landscape.

"Hey, you hillbilly commies, we're right over here."

Drew recognized the voice and the not so subtle comments. Roach sat on a plaid blanket with a cigarette in one hand, a soda in the other and large round sunglasses perched on his narrow nose. A gaunt body framed his white skin from underneath like fabric being pulled taut over a skeleton.

"What the flock," he continued, "you losers looked like you struck out the first inning with the local beach bunnies."

Howie flipped him the finger and reached for Roach's pack of cigarettes.

"Howitt, you tight ass, cheap skate, I told you to buy your own."

The round face broke into a sarcastic, arrogant smile, as he proceeded to light the cigarette. "Why should I? There's free ones right here."

"Pat, where did Red go?" Jeff questioned.

"Skip was his usual pissed off, moody self, so Red asked him to walk the beach and try to scope out some chicks. Maybe he'll lighten up sometime this century."

The guys fanned out trying to get the most strategic location for girl watching and a possible conversation with a nearby group of sun bathing babes. This whole trip was planned out for months and the expectation was to meet chicks at the shore in overwhelming numbers.

"Andy, sit down here," said Roach gesturing to an empty towel spread out nearby.

"I suppose you're going to tell me that I was here earlier and I forgot where I was sitting." Drew's tone dripped with sarcasm.

"Hey man, cool your heels!" Roach snapped at him. "We go out looking for your sorry ass early this morning and that's all you have done is bitch at us. Red told me how you've been acting like a total ass even to him."

"How would you like to have your memory spun around like a top?" Drew lashed back. "I have no idea who any of you are or what you want from me."

"Listen, just take a few more days and I know your head will clear up." Roach's tone was now more serious and direct. "We'll get you back to that clinic if you don't get any better by Wednesday. Okay, does that sound cool? But in the meantime, cut some slack because you're putting everyone on edge and ruining the start of this trip."

He reluctantly nodded.

"Okay, I'll try, but I need the answer to something." Drew hesitated not knowing if this was the right time to ask. "How do you know Andy Michaels?"

"Because dummy," Roach smiled and laughed under his breath, "he's you."

CHAPTER SIX

An early evening sun hung low in the sky still brilliant in its radiance, but losing life with each passing minute. Looking away from the boardwalk, the rays of light outlined the metal skeleton-looking frame of the roller coaster and Ferris wheel rising above the stands and buildings of Playland. The boardwalk was now switching from its daytime mode as a child's theme park to an adult Disneyland. Families still touted young children around, pushing bulky metal strollers and carriages through the throng of people, but suddenly they seemed to be in a hurry to leave and escape the emerging wild creatures of the night. No, it wasn't prowling hordes of wild dogs or wolves threatening the safety of these helpless humans. In their eyes, the packs of teenagers posed a much greater fright. Emerging from every corner, clusters of them began to swell along the length of the boardwalk.

The boys from Columbus weren't any different. They joined in the festive atmosphere alive with the jostling, carefree, fun-filled attitude only a teenager could enjoy. Skin red and sore from staying on the beach longer than they should have didn't make any difference. Each one of them knew the only reason for this trip to the shore was to get a tan and score with as many chicks as possible. Now, they were taking in the pleasures of the boardwalk nightlife certainly not to get a suntan, but to meet girls.

"I can't believe all the tough looking chicks around here," Red mumbled to the rest of his friends as they made their way past Parker's Original Ocean Taffy Shop.

"I told you guys it would be unbelievable tonight," Roach spoke up. "Last night was quiet because it was Sunday and people were heading back home. But start the week and here we go, wall to wall babes."

"Hey, you with that great tan covering that wicked-looking body want to check out my room." Howie was never one to be tactful or bashful. His usual line was very direct and to the point. The attractive blonde looked at him in disgust while indicating with a raised middle finger how she felt.

"I think she's interested," said Howie in a rather serious tone.

"Yeah, Howitt, she wants you," returned Jeff. "She wants you to get the hell out of town."

"C'mon, Howitt, you red-neck commie, all these girls are going to know what you're like and we won't have a chance to meet anyone." Roach spoke like the experienced member of the group. "They want to meet cool guys, not some hippie freak."

"Hey, you with the great buns, I bet they'll look better with my hands on them." Howie's comment fired at the next passing girl obviously showed he didn't hear Roach's advice, or didn't care.

"Okay, time to split forces," Red joined in. "I'm heading toward the pier at the south end, if anyone wants to come along."

Roach and Skip moved in Red's direction. Jeff and Reegs decided to stick with Howie, so someone wouldn't kill him out of annoyance. Drew stood by himself undecided what to do next.

A Lasting Summer

"You're with us," Roach directed his words at Drew.

He followed the three boys without a word. His walk was a mechanical stride, his brain in a numb stupor. Some realization was helping him to piece together the facts. He was in Ocean Heights, in Maryland, and it was August 1965. Those were the easy things. Who he was in this whole scenario was freaking him out. Drew was struggling with the idea that in some bizarre, unexplainable manner he was reliving his father's life back when he was a teenager. At this moment, everyone around him perceived Drew as sixteen year-old Andy Michaels. He couldn't understand how this ever could happen and a possible explanation wasn't even possible. His panic thoughts swirled through a maze of figuring out how he was going to get out of this incredible mess.

They continued walking, soaking up the lights, sounds and sights of the boardwalk nightlife. Drew noticed more of the things around him. The music was a mix of the old California beach and surf songs to the soulful Motown melodies. He often heard the oldies radio station his stepfather listened to wondering how anyone could ever listen to such garbage. He didn't recognize any of the songs or musicians by name, but many sounded vaguely familiar. One good thing, the food back in 1965 was pretty much the same. The guys had decided to eat dinner on the boardwalk. Drew followed Red, Skip and Roach to a pizza stand. The only thing he found different was that the slices of pizza were much larger and a whole lot cheaper.

As they ate, he had more of a chance to get to know the enigmatic Skip. Unlike the others, he was rather sullen and kept to himself. At times he was pretty outgoing and then would sink inward not offering any conversation. Drew didn't make much of it since he wasn't doing much talking either because he had no clue to what was going on. Skip was the shortest and skinniest of the group. His light brownish hair, light skin, pale gray eyes and fine features gave him a washed out look almost befitting his personality.

Drew began noticing the way the girls were dressed. Most of them seemed to wear their hair long and very straight. He didn't know so many appeared with blond hair because the fashion for girls was to bleach your hair, taking on that California surfing look. Shorts, halter-tops, Capri pants were all the rage. The boys wore their hair in long waves across their foreheads with blonde streaks running through them. Hawaiian print or wide vertical stripe shirts worn open and loosely draped over madras shorts, while loafers with no socks was the only way to be seen in public. The guys had chattered about what to wear before heading out, changing their outfits at least three times. Despite his protests about going out, Drew had been told he wasn't dressed properly for a night on the boardwalk. So, with Roach's help, he was given the right combination of clothes.

"I can't believe these chicks around here," Red babbled, "I never want to go home!"

"Yeah, home," Drew thought. "How am I ever going to get back?" His next move was a complete mystery.

They had traveled away from Playland reaching the end of the lighted shops and stands. The crowd was thinning out, so Red decided to backtrack toward their other friends. They had seen plenty of girls grouped together in all sorts of numbers. About half way back, they spotted Jeff and Reegs talking to a cluster of four girls. Jeff was perched on the boardwalk railing and Reegs was leaning on it. Both boys seemed to be laughing and joking with the girls.

A Lasting Summer

Jeff spotted the rest of his friends and waved them over.

"Guys, this is Donna, Gina, Sue and Lisa from New Jersey."

Introductions were made and the conversation took off from there. After ten minutes of small talk about where they were staying and where they came from, someone noticed Howie missing.

"Where is that fat, lard-ass Howitt?" questioned Roach. "That commie bastard probably defected on a fishing boat headed out to sea."

"He hooked up with a tuna," Reegs returned.

"What do you mean by a tuna?" one of the girls asked.

The boys laughed at the term used to describe Howie's not so desirable choice of girls. "I think she was swimming upstream to spawn and he was following," somebody added to the conversation.

Drew was on the edge of the conversation and on the fringe of the group. He didn't care he was back in 1965 because what these guys were doing was so stupid and a waste of time. Even if he were back at home, he would never bother to hang out talking about stupid things or trying to impress girls. He couldn't believe his father would want do these things. Maybe his father was weirder than he knew. Acting like this, dressing like these freaks, or even wanting to come to the shore to hang out with a bunch of guys seemed so useless. It was probably better he never knew his father because he might still be talking or acting like some surfing jerk.

The ebony tentacles of night had already captured the boardwalk. Slowly moving into their deep shadows, Drew began to move away from the group. He quickly blended into the mass of people wandering along the boardwalk. He wasn't quite sure where he was heading or what he hoped to find, but he needed to be away from these guys.

Drew might have been walking for hours for all he knew. The appearance of the crowd and the surroundings hardly changed, but something was different as he approached the overpowering glare and sounds of Playland. The theme park stretched out further than he had remembered from the morning. It was only a few hours earlier, yet it seemed like an eternity when all this confusion began. Staring at the rides, lights and commotion of the huge sprawling amusement park, he was certain it was far from being an illusion. Last night, it was nothing more than an abandoned collection of dilapidated buildings waiting to be demolished, but now it was a spectacular site. As he reached the end of the park, he realized it marked the end of the boardwalk.

Drew shifted his attention out toward the black curtain enveloping the ocean. Lights from distant outbound ships twinkled out across the vast expanse against the dark sky. His attention suddenly shifted to the pier jutting out into the water dimly lit by a few paltry light bulbs. This was the place for the start of his dilemma, for the nightmare that violated reality, for the reversal of time and events. In his mind, the malevolent skeleton of wood beckoned to him, taunting him with the mystery. He never hesitated, as he briskly walked the last fifty yards of the boardwalk to reach Reader's Pier.

There was no one else around. The water and sky surrounding the vacant structure appeared more ominous and darker than he remembered from the previous night. Mustering up some courage, he crawled through the open railings and made his way to the beams and pilings underneath. He waited a few minutes for his eyes to adjust to the darkness, hoping they could pierce the gloom.

A Lasting Summer

Nothing appeared. Drew could feel the cold rivulets of sweat running down his back. He had to make the next move.

"Hey, fisherman, are you out there tonight?"

His piercing voice broke the solitude of the night. Waves slowly washed up on the beach with only a muffled roll.

"If you can hear me, I need to talk to you!" shouted Drew with a brewing bitterness and anger. "You put me here and I want to know why you did this to me."

Nothing happened. Drew became agitated picking up scraps of driftwood or scattered rocks and tossed them as far out into the black void as he could. He was lashing out at the mysterious figure in the only way he could. It was like his life, where people weren't around when he needed them. His dead father was the start of all the problems in his life and he could never forgive him for his selfishness.

"What the hell are you yelling at boy?"

Drew jumped, startled at the high-pitched, scratchy voice coming from the shadows.

"You pissed off at someone out there. Jeez, you could wake up the dead with all that hollering"

A figure began to emerge from the gloom into the dimness of the pier lights. The hunched over shape began to form, and Drew quickly realized it appeared as an old woman. She wasn't much over five feet tall even though she was bent over. Her flowery dress looked faded and tattered, long past their newness. Spindly legs protruded from the dress and ended in a pair of unmatched sneakers. It was hard to make out her face, not only because of the darkness, but the countless wrinkles etching her features and lending to her age. A washed-out Yankee's baseball cap sat on her head with long, wiry blond hair going in every direction from beneath it. Every inch of exposed skin on her throat, fingers and wrists, was covered with a multitude of rings, bracelets, necklaces or beads. The trinkets glittered faintly in the dim lighting.

"You lost?" the lady continued. "Because you look like you belong at the Harbor Point Hotel with all those other rich kids."

"No," he mumbled hoping the appearing figure had been someone else. "I was just sort of looking for a guy . . ."

"I don't think anyone is going to be down here at this time of night."

"Yeah, I suppose you're right," Drew shrugged, "but I didn't have anywhere else to go to look for him."

"Who are you looking for?"

"Some guy dressed like a fisherman. He kind of just appeared out of the mist last night."

The old lady broke into a sarcastic laugh. "Do you really want me to believe that story?"

"I didn't think you would believe me." Drew stared at her. "So why did I even bother to tell you?"

"Maybe because you don't have any friends to help you," she fired back.

"I have plenty of friends. So mind you own business, and besides, what are you doing down here?"

"Oh, just taking a little stroll along the beach," replied the old woman casually. "Just a little evening walk along the ocean."

"Yeah, but you're an old lady. Aren't you afraid of being here alone?"

"I never worry about that and I'm not an old lady." She chirped back indignantly. "I'm sort of a well-respected fixture around Ocean Heights."

Do crazy things like this always happen around here? Drew shook his head to try to unscramble the vision in front of him. However, his mother did talk about the many legends that were connected to this old pier.

"Lady, I just want to get out of here and go back home."

A thin smile etched across her face.

"Home is said to be where the heart is, but where has your heart been?" she asked in a very deliberate tone. "You will return home when you have found what you were always searching for."

"Quit talking in riddles." Drew said angrily. "I only want to find this fisherman, or whoever he is and get out of this place."

Drew looked out at the empty expanse of the ocean. His mind was twisted in deeper in uncertainty and confusion, and now a new fear was finding its way into his thoughts. What if this was real and he was stuck here, back in a place and time with people he knew nothing about.

The old woman's voice sounded distant, but her words were clear enough to break his pensiveness.

"Drew, the Captain will find you again when the time is right. For now find the Flower that lives on the boardwalk."

Before he could utter a single word she was gone. Her final message made it obvious again that he was known by another mysterious figure. His mind was on the verge of panic.

CHAPTER SEVEN

Tuesday, August 9, 1965

It's often said that the ocean is like a perpetual clock, never affected by the day, the week or even the year. Tides rise and fall on a schedule connected only with the harmony of the moon's rotation around the earth. Eons of time have passed, and whether witnessed by humans or not, the rolling waves of water have endlessly risen and fallen across countless beaches.

Drew stared at the outgoing tide. It washed up to the wooden uprights of a lifeguard tower, but now with its energy fading, the water moved steadily away. He sat sprawled on a small, faded blanket mesmerized by the sheer power of the ocean and its incredible rhythm. A long, restless night with fragments of intermittent sleep made Drew leave the cottage at the first signs of dawn. Quietly, he left the rest of the boys sleeping and walked down to the beach alone. An hour later he was lost in his thoughts, as he pieced together the events from the night before.

Yesterday had been an absolute disaster muddled by more mystery and unbelievable circumstances. Last night proved to blur the situation even more with his trip to the fishing pier and run in with the old lady. Her gibberish made no sense, but somehow she knew his name and the fisherman, so he hadn't imagined him. Then, what did she

A Lasting Summer

mean about finding some flower growing on the boardwalk? Suddenly he recalled the same remark the fisherman also had made about a flower. What was this flower thing that both these people mentioned?

He did remember that hadn't even made it to the top of the pier when Red and Skip found him. Despite his arguments, they assured him that there was no old, hunched-over, strangely dressed woman emerging from below the pier. How could they have missed her? It was becoming baffling that he was the only one ever encountering these strange figures.

The rest of the night went the way it started. The guys eventually met up, then spent the rest of the time talking about the girls they had met along the boardwalk. Whether they were telling the truth or not didn't matter to him. It was sort of funny to hear their stories. Howie continued to outdo everyone else, as he was quick to say that he managed to take one willing girl underneath an isolated section of the boardwalk that jutted out toward the beach. He described his making out and trying for more with the girl when they were interrupted by the beach patrol. With taunts and mocking from the other guys, Howie didn't admit he was lying, but he stopped making out with the girl for another reason. It seems that he had left his protection in another pair of shorts, so he didn't want to risk spending the rest of his life being a father and living in some Ocean Heights trailer park.

Drew was dumbfounded with the other stories and conversations he was hearing. These guys talked endlessly about school, the neighborhood, girls, other friends from back home, sports, cars, the Beatles, the Beach Boys, Motown, and always the fun of being down here together and on their own. He wasn't sure of the things they were describing, but they were patient and he was starting to catch on. Still, he was reluctant to accept his predicament.

He stared at the receding water. The wet sand drying in the heat of the morning sun as the tide pulled away. Some people were strolling along the beach, as birds glided overhead against a deep blue sky. It was the beginning of another perfect day at the Maryland shore. Maybe, this was the very scene his father had experienced thirty-five years ago he wondered.

"No, no!" his mind screamed in silence. He fought the urge to even think like this, because then he would be accepting what was happening. Drew was cringing at the idea that he was actually reliving his deceased father's past life.

His brain shifted frameworks. He went back to the slender thread of hope that he discovered last night. True, he wasn't able to contact his mother, his aunt, or anyone else, but these guys would be heading back home come Sunday morning and he would be going with them. Today was Tuesday, so in five days he would be out of this mess and going home to Columbus. He could hold out.

"Just count the hours until Sunday," he thought, "just get through this nightmare."

Drew lay back on the narrow blanket. He folded his hands behind his head and lowered his borrowed sunglasses staring up at the cloudless sky. Sleep began to envelope his senses, as the distant solution began to seem more realistic. "I don't need to rely on anybody for help. I can do this myself," were his last fading thoughts as he drifted into a black void.

Another day on the beach and what could be any better. She carried a cloth bag slung over her shoulder filled with all the necessary things for spending the day along the ocean. People visiting the area often thought that just because you lived in a town like Ocean Heights you would be down to the beach everyday. This was hardly the case.

She, like most of her friends, worked a seasonal job available in so many of the boardwalk shops and stands. Six days of the week she sat staring out the plate glass window of the air-conditioned boutique watching the tourists romp in the crashing surf or sprawled out on their beach blankets. Her hours often varied between day and night, but she longed to just have the time to go to the beach whenever she felt. Of all the places she had lived over the past sixteen years, this was the one she liked the most. Sure, it was a summer tourist haunt with all the commotion and semblance of one giant amusement park, yet it was so exciting. The nights walking the boardwalk with her friends, then spending some part of the daytime week on the beach were things that few people could ever hope. For the past three years, since her father had been stationed here, she loved Ocean Heights more and more each day.

Tori found an isolated spot not far from the lifeguard tower. It was only midmorning and most of the tourists were either sleeping in or still eating breakfast on the strip. She didn't need to be to work until five o'clock, so she basically had the whole day to herself. Most of her friends were working, but she was looking forward to just hanging out on the beach alone, if that ended up to be the case. That possibility was probably not going to happen, since she had mentioned to her best friend, Kelli, her plans of going to the beach for the day. She knew Kelli would be in summer school at least until twelve-thirty, but knowing her friend, she probably would be here earlier. That was why she chose this spot on the beach, the same location where they would always meet up.

"Hey, girl, you could have at least waited for me."

Tori didn't even have to look up as she was spreading out her blanket. "Kelli, you are supposed to be in summer school, in geometry class, with mister whatever his name is. You can't keep cutting your classes."

"Maybe whatever his name is will not even know I'm missing, since he doesn't really know whatever my name is anyway."

Both girls laughed as they hugged in the warm embrace of two good friends. They had been together walking the boardwalk with a group of other locals last night, but they always were so glad to be together again.

"You know, Tori, we have to take advantage of the summertime and not being in real school all day long," Kelli joked. "Besides, this could be the day when we meet that perfect guy, you know, the man of our dreams."

"Yeah, sure thing Kell, said Tori, "with the boy who is visiting the shore for the week who thinks his mission is to score with every local girl he can get his grimy hands on."

"That's the one. Why, have you run into him already today?"

Both girls broke into hysterical laughs at the standing joke and the situation they knew they would soon be encountering. Not that they went out looking for any special male attention, but their stunning looks were like magnets. Tori's dark auburn hair shaped a near perfect face matched with the bluest eyes imaginable. Her tall slender body was deeply tanned more quickly than others because of her naturally darker skin. A lithe, shapely body ended with long legs seemed to catch the most male attention. She never understood why her legs drew the most comments,

A Lasting Summer

since she always felt boys were more interested in other parts of the female anatomy.

Kelli in her own way was just as attractive. A few inches shorter than her friend, Kelli had long, straight blond hair, freckles and beautiful hazel eyes. Very shapely, she carried the sculptured, muscular frame of an athlete. She excelled in three sports at school and was an all-star in every one. Colleges were already contacting her, but they could only offer her a little assistance since most of the athletic scholarship money went to the boys. The college coaches were encouraging her to play at the schools nevertheless, because they were in a legal fight to bring parity to women's athletics. In a few more years, they might be on par with the male sports. Kelli listened to their positive words, but she had another problem. Even though she dominated on the playing fields, she struggled in the classroom. She realized academically she was not even close to Tori's incredible intelligence. Kelli had the ability to at least pass, but she hated her boring classes, so she never did homework and generally blew off school. Someday, she told herself, she would get serious and become a conscientious student. For now it was the summer, the beach, and the boardwalk.

"Thanks for being here with me," said Tori affectionately. "It's always a treat hanging out with you."

"Same here," returned Kelli. "We have to take advantage of the situation now because who knows what next summer will bring. Our senior year in high school and then off to bigger and better things."

"Sure, college," Tori pensively said, "but, maybe other things too."

"Hey, don't worry about that. You'll still be here, probably longer than you think."

Tori only nodded in silence.

"Besides, you're going to be my maid of honor, when I find the right guy someday. So, don't think you're going anywhere too soon."

"Okay." Tori again hugged her closest friend, but this time with more urgency.

An hour latter, the two girls were dozing to the tunes of station WJAC and the familiar ranting of disc jockey, Jack The Mack Knife. The mix of beach sounds started to blend together. Banter from varied radio stations streaming from a multitude of transistor radios, screaming children, scolding mothers, and warning calls from the lifeguard tower began to disrupt the solitude of the early morning beach setting. It was almost noon. Kelli sat up on the blanket annoyed by the screeching from some nearby children.

"Yep, makes me want to have a bunch of those," Kelli said to no one in particular.

Tori also sat up awakened to the noise and her friend's words.

"What did you say, Kelli, you're going to try and have some kids tonight? Gee, I didn't know things were heating up between you and Eddie."

"No way, girl," Kelli shot back, "just friends and no fooling around there."

"I wonder about you two."

"Speak about wondering, what about you and Jason. Everyone knows he has a thing for you, and he is kind of cute and sexy in his own way."

"Take that back!" Tori fired a disarming look at her friend. "He's just another out-of-town guy trying to score with all the locals. His only difference is he's staying down here eight weeks instead of the usual one-week, so he has more time to work the locals."

A Lasting Summer

"Sorry, sorry, I didn't mean to twist you into a knot. I was just trying to give cupid some help."

Tori smiled not being able to stay mad very long with her friend. "No, I don't expect cupid will be visiting me none too soon. Falling in love is just a fantasy, a thing in books and movies. I'm happy just the way I am. Want to head to the pavilion for something to eat?"

"No thanks, I'm just going to stay here and relax."

Tori rose from the blanket brushing off sand from her legs. "Stay out of trouble and hold off all those cute guys."

"Sure thing," Kelli replied, "I'll save them for you."

It was no more than a five minute walk from where she had left Kelli to the pavilion. The sand was getting hotter under her feet as she trudged towards the dunes. She wished she had been a little more resourceful and brought her sandals along. The hot sand, deep sand was annoying her, but not nearly as all the whistles and catcalls she was getting from the groups of boys collecting on the beach. She wasn't naïve about her attractive looks, but on the other hand she wasn't conceited. Tori was feeling embarrassed and more self-conscious with every step. If only she had brought Kelli along, she might have been more protected from the verbal onslaught.

Quite unexpectedly, she felt a tap on her shoulder. Tori turned with a pent up fury to unleash on the boy who would dare approach her out of nowhere and touch her.

"Excuse me miss, I'm a photographer with The Heights Herald." The words were spoken from an older man probably somewhere in his thirties. He had long pants, a short-sleeve shirt with no tie and a myriad of cameras and equipment bags draped over his shoulders and around his neck. His brush cut, wide-set eyes, and bulging cheeks didn't really portray him as a guy hitting on her.

"Hi," Tori spoke in a more subdued tone than she had set out to use.

"The Herald sent me on a photo assignment to film some people on the beach enjoying this great weather we've been having," he continued in a rapid fire pace. "Would you mind possibly being in a photo that might be used by the newspaper this week?"

"I guess it would be okay," Tori politely replied.

"Hey great, by the way my name is Jimmy Thompson, but I need to just get the right scene put together."

He rushed off toward the dunes preoccupied with some idea of what he wanted to photograph. Glancing back over his shoulder, he motioned with the sweep of his arm for Tori to follow him. The area he was moving toward appeared rather isolated. The sand dunes were undisturbed and almost blocked out the entire backdrop of the boardwalk. As they got closer to the dunes, Tori spotted what the photographer was drawn to, a lone figure lay sprawled on a blanket obviously too small for his muscular frame. The boy had on sunglasses, hands folded behind his head, and he was looking straight up. Either way, he was sound asleep or quite dead.

"Excuse me guy," Jimmy blurted out in a voice that probably would have woken the dead, "I'm on assignment with the local paper taking pictures of folks on the beach. Would you mind posing for a shot?"

The boy slowly sat up, stirred from the reaches of a deep sleep. He removed his sunglasses and instantly met Tori's eyes. The air rushed from her lungs and her stomach felt as if had been kicked by a mule. Her strong legs turned to rubber, and the world started spinning through eyes unable to focus any longer. She had heard all about these feelings from friends, read all the great romance novels and poems,

A Lasting Summer

but she scoffed these off as mere giddy infatuations. Here she was, Miss Rock of Gibraltar of the emotional realm, and now she was falling apart. She knew at that very moment, her life would never be the same.

"What do I have to do?" asked the boy in a flippant manner. He was responding to the question, but Drew's eyes never left the bluest eyes of the most beautiful girl he had ever seen. But, something much more was happening. The air was sparking with electricity, flares were igniting, and volcanoes were erupting. He was beyond comprehending the kinds of feelings he never knew existed inside. The events of the last few days, and even in his life up to now, suddenly vanished into the eyes of a girl he would remember forever.

"Okay, great stuff to work with," Jimmy snapped in his hurry up tone, "now, Miss, if you could just sit on this guy's blanket and buddy if you would just kneel alongside her."

Jimmy jockeyed them around trying to capture the perfect picture. "We just need one more thing. Guy, grab that water bottle and pretend to be pouring water over her head, and, Miss, you sort of make it look like you're wincing with that water hitting you."

He moved his camera so the ocean and the sunbathers on the beach provided the background for the two figures posing for a carefree outing on a beautiful summer day.

Seconds later, Jimmy clicked the shutter. A flash of light energy burned into an empty strip of film causing inert chemicals to react. These mindless molecules did their job. A captured glimpse of the present, a fleeting moment of time; they recorded an event that few would hardly remember or care about. But, for these two teenagers brought together in this chance encounter, this image cast on a lifeless piece of plastic would last forever.

"Man what a great shot!" he burst out, already packing away his camera equipment. "Listen, check Sunday's edition on the picture page and if the editors use this come down to The Herald. You'll each get ten dollars. Hey, thanks again.

He was off in a flash, gone as quickly as he had arrived. Tori couldn't gain her composure. She was rattled in a way she had never experienced before. The closeness to this unfamiliar boy had melted her down to her instincts. The combination of those striking good looks, defined muscular frame, and those ocean blue eyes. She physically just wanted to reach out and hold him in her arms. A tidal wave of emotions had taken their toll. She was literally speechless.

Drew wasn't feeling much different. His lack of any experience was evident, but suddenly to meet a girl as beautiful as this was emotionally devastating. He had no clue how to describe the feelings rushing through him.

"Weird guy," he mumbled in an unintelligible voice.

Tori weakly nodded as he stood up and started walking away. Her brilliant mind had been turned to tapioca. Words couldn't be spoken because she couldn't move her mouth.

Drew watched her leave, moving toward the mass of teenagers now gathering in larger numbers along the beach. He never asked her name because he didn't know how to ask a girl anything. She was gorgeous beyond words, and he was harboring feelings he couldn't identify. His only resolution was to believe a girl of this caliber had to have a boyfriend waiting for her further down the beach. There was no way he could even stand a chance with somebody that incredibly stunning. Then again he thought, how do you explain to someone that you're from the year 2000 and suddenly you wake up and it's 1965?

"What the heck," he thought as he gathered up the tiny blanket and decided to head back to the cottage. "The third

A Lasting Summer

astonishing person I've met since this trip back in time. The fisherman, the old wandering lady, and . . . ." There were no words to describe perfection and someone with whom you couldn't possibly believe was real.

"Tori, what's wrong with you!" Kelli shouted as her friend unexpectedly returned and she saw the condition she was in. "Did some guy say something to you? Don't tell me that creep Jason showed up?"

Tori collapsed on the blanket next to her friend. Her bronze tan was muted and her eyes glistened with tears. Flustered was a mild description of her state of mind.

"Come on," Kelli continued in a rage that was building over her friend's sudden appearance, "show me where that creep is and I'll go over and kick the crap out of him!"

"No, no," Tori finally was able to weakly mumble, "it's not what you think."

"Talk to me, Tori, you're scaring me right now. Ever since I've known you I have never seen you act like this."

"You'll never believe it if I tell you the whole truth," Tori said beginning to regain some composure and wiping the tears of happiness from her eyes.

"It better be good, because you look like a freight train just rolled over you."

The next five minutes, Tori did the best she could to elaborate all the events of the strangest thing that had ever happened to her. The chance selection by The Herald photographer, the unfamiliar boy sitting by himself, the picture, and then . . .

"I think it may have happened," said Kelli smiling in pure delight. "Oh yeah Tori, you fell instantly in love with a total stranger."

"It can't possibly happen like that," Tori resisted. "I don't know who he is, where he's from, if he's some weird psycho, or if he's down here with his girlfriend. Kell, I never even spoke to him."

"It doesn't matter. You found the guy you're supposed to be with forever. He just happened to show up in Ocean Heights and you just happened to meet him in some dumb publicity photo. For some reason fate has brought both of you together for some weird reason right here and now."

Tori lowered her head. "I don't even know his name."

Kelli put her arms around Tori trying to comfort her topsy-turvy emotions. "Listen, I'll walk back with you to where he was last and we'll talk to him together."

Moments later, Tori and Kelli arrived at the spot where the picture was taken. The boy that she couldn't get out of her head or her heart was gone.

"Tori, don't worry, we'll find him somewhere on the beach or maybe tonight on the boardwalk."

"I was so stupid not to talk to him. What if he is heading back home today? What if he wanted to meet me?" Tori brought her hands to her face in despair. "Kelli, I'll never know if this whole thing was real."

"You know I've lived here my whole life. The legends are never-ending, but there always seems to be some mysterious force working around here." Kelli tried to soothe her friend's dilemma. "I think everything will work out fine. If you believe in love, good things will happen."

Tori didn't believe a thing her friend was saying. Things in her life had never been easy or smooth, so why would they change now?

CHAPTER EIGHT

Considering the mental state he was in, Drew somehow made it back to the cottage. It could have taken minutes, days or even weeks to get there, but he couldn't remember and didn't care. The image of the girl kept flashing in his mind. This was not normal, he thought and probably more proof of his injury. Maybe he was lying somewhere in a hospital bed with needles and tubes stuck in him, machines keeping him alive, and his brain was spinning these weird scenarios. Things like this didn't even happen to him in a dream, so it had to be some extreme trauma to his body. Yet nevertheless, what if she was real and somehow he was actually feeling these unexplained emotions. Oh man, he really needed Sunday to arrive as quickly as possible.

"Hey, Andy, were you out scoping the beach for babes?" Roach sarcastically asked as Drew pulled the screen door open. He sat behind a bowl of cereal, a lit cigarette in his hand, and the sunburn on his shirtless body could have won a neon sign contest. "You know that much snatch can be very unhealthy for one person, so you should share it with your good friends."

Red sat in a worn out sofa chair with his legs, arms, shoulders, face and neck covered in a white film of Calamine lotion. His skin literally glowed from beneath the cooling salve.

Drew looked at the stricken Red. "You don't look very good," he said from his semi-trance.

"No shit, Einstein," said Roach laughingly. "I guess we stayed out a bit too long yesterday, but what the flock, it'll turn to tan sooner or later."

"What time is it?" Howie wandered out from the side bedroom.

"Past noon, Howitt, but we wanted you to sleep longer so you could be in prime condition for tuna fishing tonight."

"Screw you, hillbilly," Howie responded to the Roach's comment. "Maybe your cousins from the mountains will be here tonight for you to poke later on."

Roach flipped him the bird.

"Where did the other guys go?"

"Skip actually went with Jeff and Reegs to Ocean Drive," said Red. "They were going to have breakfast then do some shopping. They're not burned as bad as we are, but I don't think they want to lie on the beach today. They talked about just hanging around town today and then heading for the boardwalk tonight."

"Sounds good to me," Howie yawned heading toward the bedroom. "I think I'm going to catch a few more z's."

The cottage was heating up with the intense afternoon sun. They gathered a few things to eat, some magazines, a newspaper, a radio, then walked a short distance to a covered shelter perched at the upper edge of the beach near the cottages. A cooling sea breeze swirled through the shelter, keeping it comfortable while the roof blocked the painful rays of sun from reaching the boys' sensitive skin.

Drew tagged along trying to maintain a presence, but not wanting to draw any more attention than he needed. He had a thousand questions he wanted to ask them about the girl from the beach, but how do you talk to guys you don't even know. Besides, what the heck would he ask them?

Red sprawled on a comfortable-looking webbed chair, while Roach leaned over the railing of the shelter looking out towards the ocean. The ever—present cigarette dangled from his lips. Drew sat on the wooden steps of the shelter just off to the side.

"Hey, Andy," Red began, "you starting to get some of your memory back."

"Sort of," Drew lied.

"That's cool, because you have to be acting normal before we head home on Sunday."

Drew nodded his acknowledgement.

"Do you guys realize that we are going to be seniors and it's our last year in high school," Roach casually remarked. "This is it boys, one more year then college and out into the world."

"Yeah, I just hope I can get into college," Red painfully sat up grimacing in discomfort. "I want to be accepted in a good school and graduate in a field I can make some money."

"Baby, college will definitely be party time," added Roach.

"Hey, Pat, you know you can't start that stuff. If you flunk out or get low grades, you'll lose your deferment."

"I don't care. Maybe the Marines would be a better choice for me anyhow."

"What's a deferment?" Drew realized a moment too late that he probably was asking about something he should have already known.

Red quickly came to his aid. "You know, Andy, a deferment is a 2-s classification from the draft board. As long as you're in college and maintain your GPA, you can't get drafted into the army until you graduate."

"Yeah, I remember now," Drew again lied.

"No, big deal," Roach said. "The thing in Vietnam will be over before we're even close to graduating. Too bad, because I would like to be there blowing away some of those commie gook bastards."

"You really think that's going to happen?" asked Red.

"Sure thing because with our military power and weapons, we'll blow those slants back into the Stone Age," he replied.

"I was worrying about getting drafted and having to go into the army," Red mulled. "Then I would have to fight in some war in a place I never heard of before."

"You can forget about that because President Johnson will probably send in about a thousand Marines and they'll clean up the place in a month. Besides, they're not going to send guys with college degrees into a jungle to shoot it out with some stone-aged natives. All the college guys will probably go to military bases in Germany and Japan."

Drew didn't say a word. He knew from his American History class that the Vietnam War turned out to be a horrible fiasco. Thousands of Americans were killed and wounded plus the war lasted almost ten years. If he could only explain to them what was about to happen, but he knew they would never believe him. How do you just sit there, knowing what will happen in the future, but were afraid to say anything because they would really think you're crazy.

"What about you, Andy, are you still thinking of majoring in pre-med?"

Red directed his question at Drew hoping to get him to be a little more talkative. He looked better than the morning they had first found him, but he didn't seem to want to speak much. Funny, he was never like this before. He had known him since grammar school, lived in the same neighborhood, went to high school together, and did just everything with him and the rest of the guys. It seemed as if he was a person who looked just like Andy, but somehow didn't act anything like him.

Drew was startled by the question. He had never even thought about selecting a major in college other than the fact he just wanted to go away. His father had been a doctor, but he never knew that he had chosen this career so far back in his life. But why would it matter? His father wasn't around to tell him these kinds of things. Strangely, he was beginning to learn some things about his father just by listening to these guys talking.

He hesitated for a moment. "No, I probably will go into something in computer technology."

Both Pats looked at him quizzically.

"What the hell is that," Roach spoke up, "some science fiction mumble jumble?"

"Yeah, just some new area of study," Drew quickly replied trying to sidestep another one his spoken mistakes.

Roach quickly moved away from Andy's answer, not quite sure what the hell he was talking about. "Red, I think you'll end up marrying some local girl from the neighborhood, have about ten kids, and live about a block from where you live right now. Real, sort of Irish-Catholic thinking."

"Kiss off, Roach, you don't even know what you're talking about." Red tried to defend himself, but he had been dating a girl for the past six months who did live in a nearby suburb of Columbus. So, the hillbilly wasn't totally right. Roach had only been part of the group of friends for the past year, but he was uncannily observant.

"Andy, what about Skip's sister, Ann. She has always had a thing for you, but you might end up in jail if you start messing around with her now. Her mother thinks you're so perfect, I don't think she would care just to get you in the family."

"Leave him alone," Red said laughing. "You're going to make him think someone is waiting back home for him with a shotgun. Don't worry, Andy, Ann is only thirteen, but I think you could be in trouble in another three or four years."

"Why do guys waste so much time thinking about girls?" Drew's question silenced both boys.

"Did you become a fag with that concussion, or did you get your balls cut off and didn't tell us?" Roach sarcastically posed the questioned, but he was waiting for a truthful reply.

"No, I'm okay, but why the big deal about all these girls?"

"He's feeding you guys a truckload of bullshit."

All three boys turned simultaneously with the remark. None of them had noticed Skip walking in unexpectedly.

"I saw this lying bastard earlier this morning talking to the toughest looking, most amazing-body chick on this entire beach."

"You commie traitor, I should have known it was another one of your smokescreens." Roach was up and agitated. "You have the balls to tell us what the flock wasting time with chicks when you're out making it with some hot-ass babe. Well, at least we know you still have your balls."

"No, no it was really not what you think," Drew stammered, trying to defend him self. "I was just minding my own business when this guy came up and wanted to take my picture."

"Yeah, but not alone," Skip added.

"Okay, he had some girl with him to pose in the picture with me."

Skip shook his head in disbelief. "This girl was the most beautiful thing I have ever seen. They don't even have girls who look that good in Playboy."

"Red, let's drown this lying bastard right now." Roach went for Drew.

"Hold on Roach," said Red, "I think we deserve some details from our amnesia whacked friend. So, who is she?"

"I don't know!" Drew shouted out.

"What do you mean you don't know?" Skip asked. "I saw you from the boardwalk talking to her after the photographer left."

"Yeah, I did, but I didn't ask her name."

"Sure thing, Mr. Cool, hit on anything with long blond hair and killer legs," Roach sarcastically responded. "I think you're just holding out on your good friends, so we don't cut in your action."

"That's not true. I was so nervous that I didn't ask her for a name or anything."

"Man, you blew it this time," Skip laughed.

"The only thing I heard her mention to the reporter is that she is a local, whatever that is."

"Oh boy, there's big trouble with that story. These local chicks want nothing to do with any guys on vacation because they know what they're after." Roach based his explanation on the many years he had spent on the shore with his family.

"Andy, was she that nice?" Red asked his friend.

"She was absolutely incredible!" Drew surprised himself with that sudden outcry of uttered emotion. "But, I know I'll never see her again."

"The hell you won't," Red replied. "We'll walk this whole flocking boardwalk tonight until we find her."

Drew was startled by the unexpected plan of action. "You guys would do that for me?" It was a question from somewhere inside, a reaction to something no one he knew would ever have done for him. Guys his own age, suddenly calling him a friend were willing to do whatever to help him out. He was more confused now than ever. Meeting a girl, something he never would have thought was important until this moment.

"Hey, Andy," Red spoke up. "We're best friends and that means we're always there for each other, whatever it is."

She fired a quick glance out the plate glass window for probably the thousandth time that night. It had been easier when the sun was still out, but with night approaching, lights from the boardwalk were reflecting off the glass. She was having a hard time recognizing even the people she knew walking by.

"Of all the time to be scheduled to work," Tori suffered in silence. "I know I'll never see him again."

Jan's Dare to Wear Beachwear was just one of the countless shops lining the boardwalk. Tori was working her second summer at Jan's and actually enjoyed the little shop specializing in women's beach clothing. Her schedule varied during the week, so today she was working the evening shift to closing time. She kept trying to reason through her quandary. If she had worked the day shift, she never would have been on the beach. Therefore, she never would

A Lasting Summer

have been asked to be in the picture, and, she gasped, never would have met him.

His face hadn't left her thoughts for a minute since she first saw him. It was beyond being too good to be true. Simply, it was unreal. Yet now, when she should be out canvassing the boardwalk, hoping to run into him, to see him again, and get a chance to talk to him, she was trapped in the store. Tori had actually thought of calling in sick, but Jan didn't have any extra help this week, so she didn't want her boss to be stuck here all day. Maybe, just maybe, she would see him walking by, and then she could run out, ask him his name and where he was from, and how long he would be here, and . . . she just had so many questions she wanted to ask him. So far, her luck wasn't very good, and her neck was aching from twisting around every time a boy walked by.

The door opened bringing another customer in along with the sounds and smells of the boardwalk. Tori was helping a middle-aged woman and her two daughters toward the back of the shop when a familiar voice called out.

"Hey girl, the boardwalk is really hopping tonight."

Tori moved toward her best friend. "Kelli, did you see him?"

"I'm not sure," she answered, "there's a lot of cute guys out there tonight, but I don't know what I'm looking for."

The mother and her daughters indiscreetly glanced towards the two girls eavesdropping on their conversation.

"Kelli, I told you what to look for."

"Yeah, I know, like about a hundred times."

"He's just so unbelievable!"

"Sure, and so are about a dozen guys I could have picked."

Both of the young customers giggled. In their very early teens, boys were becoming a priority and they were well aware of the male sights on the boardwalk.

"Always happens that way," the mother spoke out. "The most perfect guy you'll ever want to find, and then, you never see him again."

Tori just sighed as she handed the woman her change.

"Not to be totally discouraging, just remember one thing," the woman went on, "if it's meant to be, it will be, and you'll find each other again."

A thin smile formed on Tori's face. "Thank you for the purchase and for the encouragement."

The woman and her daughters left the store. Kelli told her friend she would make another trip down the boardwalk and would come back at nine when Tori would be closing. Left with her thoughts, Tori continued to stare out the window, hoping by chance to spot him. Another customer came in. Suddenly, her knees began to wobble and her head started spinning. She could feel the blood rushing to her face. The boy entering the store was met with a hurricane.

"What do you want now?" she coldly asked.

"Hey, Tori, no need to bite. Just thought I would come over and help you close up, so we can head to Mitch's for something to eat, and maybe a few brews."

"What's this like some date request?"

"You could say that, since I left tonight open for you."

"Do me a favor, Jason. Why don't you drive up to Sandy Inlet and try making it with those girls, because they don't know you or your reputation."

"Tori, Tori," the tall, blond hair boy responded. He was muscular, athletic, and prominent chiseled features sculpted a very handsome face. His hair swept across his forehead in a characteristic surfer look. Unfortunately, his

A Lasting Summer

good looks couldn't make up for his arrogant, egotistical, pompous attitude. Generally, he felt any girl could be his to do whatever he wanted.

"Why do you have to be so nasty to me when I just want to make you special."

"Give me a break," said Tori sarcastically. "You just want another notch in your belt, but sorry it won't happen here with me."

"I think if you just went out once or twice with me, you'll see how good it can really be."

Tori was just about to speak out when a crash of thunder rattled the front window.

"Oh shit," Jason burst out, "I left the top down on my convertible. Damn weatherman never said anything about rain tonight."

Without another word, Jason sprinted out the store much to Tori's satisfaction. She was getting awful tired of having to deal with him almost everyday. He was confident that he would take her out and his approach was typical of his overbearing personality. Jason would persistently wear out the opposition, so the reluctant girl would eventually give into his demands. Tori was determined that this jerk would leave Ocean Heights without ever being with her. The problem was, he had been here three weeks already and probably would be here to Labor Day, which was almost four more weeks away.

Tori opened the front door allowing the air-conditioning to escape into the humid, thick air. The boardwalk was jammed with people, but a sudden flash of lightning and another crash of thunder started a wild scurry. Seconds later, the thick, black sky seemed to split open like an over-ripe fruit releasing a downpour of heavy, drenching raindrops. Anyone not already moving seemed to be swept up in the cascading water as they scurried for the protection of cars and buildings. One figure seemed to outrun even the rain, but as Kelli approached, her hair was matted to her face and her clothes soaked through.

"No cruising the boardwalk tonight." Kelli wiped the water from her face. "Sorry, but maybe we can find him tomorrow on the beach."

"Sure thing," Tori replied dejectedly, as she locked the front door from the inside, flicked off the display lights and headed toward the back service door to leave. "As that woman said earlier, if it's meant to be, it'll happen no matter what."

"Sorry, Andy, but I think we're finished for tonight," Red spoke out as they huddled under the canvas awning of Crocker's Clam Stand. He was there with Drew, Roach, Howie, Jeff and Reegs. Skip had wandered off alone in another direction. The guys had walked the entire length of the boardwalk at least a half a dozen times hoping to find the girl Andy had described. Even though their search was futile, they had enjoyed the night, cavorting with groups of girls along the way. Drew remained reserved, going along with whatever the guys were doing, but lost entirely in the thoughts of the girl. He kept thinking that even though she was a local, he probably would never find her again before they left on Sunday. Earlier this morning, Sunday seemed like a million years away. Suddenly, it now was coming too soon.

The boys had been encouraging all night trying to keep his spirits up. The unexpected rain had trashed any hope for finding her tonight. These guys were so great, he thought. If they indeed were his father's friends, he was really lucky to have had them. Drew peered out toward the black ocean and the sheet of falling rain, wondering if the mysterious fisherman was at sea tonight. The guys huddled closer, just barely having reached the protective shelter. Crocker's Clam Stand stood for the past six years a scant three stores away from Jan's Dare to Wear Beachwear.

CHAPTER NINE

Wednesday, August 10, 1965

A gray, murky sliver of light seeped through the edges of the blinds. The thin strips of plastic, victimized so many mornings by the cutting shards of a brilliant rising sun, were now in total control of the paltry, feeble bits of light trying desperately to enter the darkened room. In the dim shaded room, the sleeping figures were hardly distinguishable, but their silhouettes were outlined by the contrasting shades of black and gray. The muffled patter of raindrops drifted through the open window. It was a soft, pleasant almost tranquilizing sound that just made a person want to stay in bed.

Drew glanced at the prone shapes of the two boys. He knew Pat and Roach had no intentions of getting up. Sneaking a quick glance at the clock radio, the illuminated numbers projected a seven-fifteen number combination. No way were these guys going to be stirring. Lifting the gym bag from alongside his bed, he moved through the darkened hallway toward the bathroom. It was obvious he was the only one in the cottage awake. Ten minutes later, he had showered and dressed as quietly as possible, not wanting to disturb the sleeping boys.

Seated alone at the kitchen table, he sipped a glass of orange juice he had poured from the refrigerator. His mind

A Lasting Summer

began to wander, as it had so many countless times to the girl from the beach. Drew was frustrated with their failed attempt to locate her last night, and even more annoyed their efforts were cut short by the rain and lightning. His hopes were fading of ever finding her again.

Suddenly, reality crashed into him like a freight train. He shook his head in disbelief for forgetting about what was even going on here. This was probably a dream, so nothing would ever be real. Why was he even thinking this could be a possibility?

Another contradiction blazed into his mind. He looked down at the unfamiliar clothes he was now wearing. But could they really be his father's? He remembered the times growing up when at school or around the neighborhood, boys would strut around wearing an old team jacket, hunting coat, or anything else their father used to wear. Growing into your father's clothes was a sign of maturing, getting older, and bragging this up to the kids around you. Unfortunately, Drew never had the chance to brag.

It was becoming sort of weird. He was beginning to experience something he thought was impossible. Deep inside, Drew started to feel a connection to a father he had never known. It was strange, but things were somehow creeping into his life. Maybe not clearly, but a tiny flicker of light peered through the darkness. As long as he could remember, he just wanted to be able to know his father in a way differently than the way people talked about him. His frustration of never knowing had smoldered to a higher temperature, igniting his bitterness and anger toward people around him.

"These clothes might have been his," he thought, still not quite sure what it all meant. The things in this bag were probably important to him, and perhaps a part of his life.

An unexpected calm settled over him. Years of doubt, confusion, and turmoil could never be purged by this single realization, but it was the first positive step in the labyrinth of emotions that had poisoned him for so long. It was as if a ray of sunlight had pierced the bleakness of his existence, giving him a hope and direction he had sought while growing up. His mother was a tremendous person, he knew for sure. She was a warm, caring woman always there for him, but she could only fill the void so much. Something tugged at his heart. He never realized how much he loved his mother until now. Burying his face in his hands, he began to understand that learning so many things about his father was opening up feelings inside he never experienced before. Was his father reaching out from somewhere and guiding him, touching his life in some unexplainable manner?

An hour passed with Drew immersed deeper in his attempts to understand the situation. These guys, Pat and Roach, and Jeff and Howitt, and the rest were maybe actually part of his father's life. They all seemed to mean so much to each other. Everything they did, they did together. Every single, little thing was amplified and enhanced by the power of their group. They seemed to feed off each other's energy helping to diminish their individual weakness and faults, but magnifying their strengths. By themselves, they would be lost. Together, they were taking full advantage of their unity, closeness, and youth.

He dug deeper into the bag, almost in an attempt to search more into his father's life. A paperback book, *Arrowsmith*, by some guy called Sinclair Lewis sat on top a couple of magazines. Drew never heard of this book, but then again he rarely read anything. He turned the book over, curious as to what it might be about. The jacket outline read, "*Martin Arrowsmith is a boy growing up in small Midwest town who pursues his dream to become a doctor."* His father had a novel describing the life of a physician, something he would someday become. Another clue to his father's existence: this is what he always wanted to be.

Two magazines piled together were *Sports Illustrated* and *Field and Stream*. So, maybe his father liked sports and maybe he fished. These were things Drew would have loved to been involved in, but a mother can only do so much. He knew he had some athletic ability, at least his gym teachers always told him, but how can you learn anything, like throwing a ball or catching a football, without a father around. Fishing seemed so neat. He liked to watch the fishing shows on cable and maybe try it someday, yet the same problem existed.

Tucked under another layer of clothes, Drew found a black wallet. The leather was soft, but well worn and used. He hesitated for a moment, not quite sure if it was appropriate to look into something that personal. Well, if it was only a dream, why not. He removed a pile of bills, mostly tens and fives with a few twenties totaling to one hundred and twenty-five dollars. Not very much money he figured, but then again everything seemed to be so much cheaper than back home, back in the present time. The smaller pockets of the wallet held what appeared to be cards. He slipped an ID card out with Bishop Simmons High School printed in bold red letters along the top. The picture looked as if he was staring at himself in a mirror. Andrew Michaels was the name typed underneath. No wonder everyone mistakenly referred to him with his father's name.

Another pocket held a folded picture whose edges were chipped and tattered. Obviously it meant something to his father because it was hidden away. Drew opened the aging photo. It was younger version of his father standing with his arm around an even younger girl. The black and white picture only revealed a very cute, attractive blond girl who appeared to be excited to be there. Drew twisted the photo over and a smudged, blue-pen sentence stretched across the back. "Andy, someday I'll be ready for you. Love, Ann." Drew smiled at the picture.

"Hey, Dad, mom wouldn't appreciate knowing about this."

"You eat breakfast yet?"

The voice startled Drew causing him to drop the keys back into the bag. Jeff stood in the doorway from his bedroom in a pair of gym shorts and nothing else. His tussled hair and drooping eyes revealed his semi-awake state.

"No, I just had a glass of orange juice."

Jeff moved toward the refrigerator, opening the door. He bent over searching for anything that wasn't moving and appearing edible. Two slices of cold pepperoni pizza emerged in one hand and a bottle of Pepsi in the other.

"Breakfast of champions," he mumbled.

Drew sat across the kitchen table with a person he was supposed to know, but in all reality was a total stranger to him.

"What do you think about all this Andy?"

"About?"

"Being down here at the shore with the guys and having no parents around."

"Yeah, pretty cool," Drew responded.

"I never thought we could pull this off," continued Jeff, "but Roach convinced my mother and Reeger's parents that everything would be fine."

A Lasting Summer

Jeff broke into a mischievous laugh with an equally twinkle in his eyes. "Well, we were going to meet Roach's family who were supposedly vacationing down here."

"Yeah, real neat," was all Drew could manage.

"Hey, Andy, was that shore chick really as hot as Skip said?"

Drew took a deep breath. This was a direct question about something he was trying to avoid. What came out his mouth next would be a confession of his inner feelings. "She was nothing like I could ever imagine existing."

Jeff's expression couldn't hide his amazement. "You think she's the real deal?"

"What do you mean?"

"Was she the girl you would want to be with the rest of your life?"

Drew hesitated, pondering the question and thought about something he had never considered possible to him.

"I am not sure," he replied knowing his face was turning red from embarrassment, "because I don't really know her, yet."

"Seems sort of unusual that you're that interested," Jeff said. "Every girl back home wants to go out with you, but you just sort of slide by, not bothering with any of them."

"I do?"

A twisted, mocking laugh poured out of Jeff. "You lying bastard, you know you're like that!"

Drew squirmed in his chair. He needed to change the subject quickly.

"So, do your parents really believe everything you told them about this trip?"

It was Jeff's turn to hesitate. A brief, silent moment passed by.

"I'm not sure they even care."

It wasn't the answer he was expecting, but Jeff's pained look forced him to continue listening.

"Since their divorce, they both just sort of do their own thing. I guess they figure my sisters and I can manage because we're older now. I still can't get use to not having my dad around, even though I see him every other weekend."

Drew related to the boy's despair. Still, his father was around and he had a chance to know him as a person. Just as quickly as the bitterness rose to the surface in Drew, another realization crept into thoughts. Jeff seemed unhappy about his parent's situation, but in fact, he appeared pretty normal and content. Maybe other kids went through a dilemma similar to his. They were hurt and saddened, but they appeared able to deal with it better than he. Had he judged his father and his death too harshly over all the years?

"You guys are up pretty early to be shooting the shit." John Reeger slowly staggered into the kitchen, still not quite awake. "You guys planning what to do today?"

"Not much going to happen with that rain," said Jeff motioning toward the gloom piercing the window.

Drew's emotional state deflated a bit more knowing that finding the girl would be impossible today. His only hope was walking the beach or boardwalk and coming across her by sheer luck. Unless the rain stopped, the beach would probably remain deserted.

John Reeger poured a glass of orange juice and leaned up against the counter. "I just want to be out cruising and looking for chicks."

"Hey, did you already forget about Becky?" Jeff asked. "You've only been going out with her the past five months."

"Yeah, she's okay," Reeger responded, "but these are gorgeous girls down here who just want lots of special attention."

"Love and leave them, right Reegs."

Howie entered the kitchen and conversation all at the same time. "That's my motto."

"Kiss off, Howitt," said Jeff, "you act that way because every girl dumps your ass after they spend an hour talking to you."

Howie flipped him a middle finger as he lit a cigarette up.

"You have to come all the way down here because every girl back at school won't even bother looking at you. New territory till the word gets out on the street."

"Too bad you queers don't want to associate with me then," Howie arrogantly spoke up, "because I have some new leads and places to visit."

"Yeah, some senior citizen's home is having a dance tonight." Reeger's comment caused everyone to starting laughing.

"Kiss my butt," Howie returned hardly daunted by the mocking comments he was so used to hearing.

"Last night on the boardwalk, I stopped in the game room at Playland," he began. "Well before long, these two scummy locals started telling me about the action along the boardwalk. The chicks get used to being hit on all the time, so any chance of scoring with them is slim to none."

"Like that's news to us," said Jeff.

Howie continued. "These two dudes were actually pretty cool after awhile. They told me about this place in Bayside called The Inferno. It's sort of like a bar with a live band that's always packed, especially with the hottest local chicks. Not many tourists know about it because it's in

Bayside, so the locals dig not having guys just being here a week and then running off."

"So, we're not?"

"Sure we are, but they probably think we don't know about this bar, so why not drop in and pretend we live further up the coast."

Nobody said a thing. With the exception of Drew, they were all there on the same mission.

"Okay, but how do we get there? Jeff asked. "Bayside is about forty miles north of us."

"These two guys, Spider and Cody, have a car and said they would take me and any of my friends who wanted to go."

"What's the catch," Reeger spoke out. "Are they fags or something?"

"No, they're cool, but they're skinny, little odd-balls who are always getting harassed by a group of Boston preppies spending the summer down here. They need some protection, and they think the more guys they come in with the better it will be for them."

"Might be a good night to go there," said Jeff, "since the weather is going to keep us off the boardwalk anyway."

Reegs nodded his approval of the plan. Howie was automatically in.

"What about it, Andy?"

Drew's mind was collapsing around the idea. He wanted to spend every minute he could on the beach looking for her, but the rain stymied that possibility. Now, this trip to Bayside would keep him and the guys off the boardwalk tonight. Another day lost, and his hope was desperately fading away.

"Sure, why not." Drew again surprised himself. He was going along with the guys mostly because he wanted to be

A Lasting Summer

with them. In a few short days, he was beginning to believe he was an accepted member of a group of guys. "I'm going out for awhile."

Twenty minutes later, Drew was perched over the boardwalk railing scanning an almost deserted beach. With Jeff, Reegs and Howie returning to bed, he had just about sprinted to the boardwalk hoping for the impossible. The rain tumbled softly and lazily from the gray clouds dampening his clothes, but more so his spirits. He was so infatuated by her he thought he might be able wish her to appear. If this was actually a dream, why couldn't he try to insert her image, make her materialize.

Maybe it was just the frustration or the futility of the situation, but Drew reached down into himself and grasped for something he never had acknowledged before. Barely whispering, the words formed on his lips.

"Dad, if you can hear me now, please help me."

The rain picked up driving Drew towards the shops along the boardwalk. He idly wandered along darting in and out of overhanging awnings and roofs. Some of the stores and boutiques were already opened, but the tourist crowd was hardly out. He was nearing the end of the business section as the shops were getting smaller and less obvious. Drew was paying little attention to the store displays, until a strange assortment of crystal balls, zodiac symbols, and mystic sketches filled the window of 'Fortunes from the Sea.'

Drew stood in front on an obscure little shop tucked away between a rundown clothing store and a gaudy souvenir stand. He walked into the dim, gray light filling the small shop. Incense aromas from a couple of tiny candles floated through the confines of the small interior. Thick, brocaded drapes hung from the ceiling and continued around the walls. A small table was positioned in the middle of the tiny room with two ornate chairs facing each other. There was nothing on the table. No crystal ball or mysterious artifact that he thought every fortune-teller would have. An almost unnoticeable business card lay on the table. Drew squinted in the dim light trying to make out the scripted gold lettering.

Madam Rosalie Zahrah
Reader of Fortunes and Savior to the Lost

He was at the point of bursting into a cheer. Why didn't he think of this before? A fortune-teller would know all about mysterious things and probably be able to explain everything. What he was doing here? Who was this fisherman? How could he get home? He had a thousand questions spinning through his head, but suddenly everything came to a screeching halt. His thought locked on to the most important thing at this moment. Who was that girl from the beach? But more importantly, would he ever see her again?

"Excuse me, can I help you?"

Drew spun towards the voice coming from behind him. A girl not much older than him stood in a small opening in the curtains. Her long black hair was pulled back in a ponytail. Fine, delicate features graced a beautiful Arabic face of olive skin set with the most piercing dark eyes he had ever seen. Her slender frame was covered with an over-sized tee shirt and a pair of faded jeans. Unexpectedly, she stood there with a broom in one hand and a dustpan in the other.

"Are you the fortune-teller?" Drew asked.

A Lasting Summer

The girl held back from laughing out hysterically.

"Do I really look like a teller of fortunes and revealer of the future?"

"No, I guess not," he apologized. "Sorry I bothered you."

"Wait a minute," she quickly returned, "what were you expecting to see?"

"I kind of thought, fortune-tellers are a lot older and they dress in all kinds of fancy robes with things in their hair, and bracelets and rings all over their fingers."

"So, I am just some cleaning woman in your opinion."

"No, I didn't mean that, it's just that you are kind of young and plain looking, and . . ."

"Okay, stop right there before you put your foot deeper into your mouth."

The girl smiled reaching to shake his hand.

"Hi, my name is Jonne."

"Hello, I'm Drew," he hesitated for a moment, "but my friends call me Andy."

It seemed so natural to use the name he hated so much.

"That's a funny name," Drew continued surprised at how easy it was to talk to this girl.

"Well you do realize I am of Arabic descent, so it's a very ancient name given to me by my mother from generations before her." She sat down on one of the chairs and offered Drew the other.

"I suppose you're looking for Madam Zahrah, the real fortune-teller," Jonne said. "Well you're out of luck because she took the day off knowing the rain would keep all the tourists away. I am just here to clean the shop and stock the shelves in the back."

"Oh, so she won't be here later?" Drew dejectedly asked.

"No, I am sorry, but you do look disappointed." The girl reached for his hand. "Are you in some kind of trouble?"

Drew was scared to tell her the mess he really was in and why he wanted to see a fortune-teller. He knew she would think he was crazy.

"I guess I'm just going to head back to my cottage," said Drew avoiding her question as he moved from the chair. "I might come back tomorrow and talk to her."

"Okay," Jonne mentioned, "I will tell her to expect a boy named, Andy."

Standing at the door, Drew turned towards the girl.

"Jonne, do you know about a special flower that grows on the boardwalk?"

"Nothing on the boards except sand and tourists," she laughed in response. "Why do you ask?"

"Just something people told me to look for."

"I think they were playing a joke on you."

"Yeah," Drew mumbled as he walked out the door, "just another stupid joke on me."

Nine guys jammed into a car heading to Bayside. Drew was looking at the impossible, but the Oldsmobile 1961 Stratocruiser station wagon easily handled three in the front seat, four squeezed in the back seat, and two seated backwards in the rear compartment on a fold-up seat. The big Olds cruised along with the scruffy-looking Spider behind the wheel, the radio blasting away, and a few of the boys engaged in some type of conversation.

The day had been very uneventful and actually pretty boring. The rain front had settled over Ocean Heights for most of the day keeping the beach and boardwalk just about

A Lasting Summer

empty from any activity. No one wanted to hang around the cottage with nothing to do, so unanimously, the guys had agreed to make the trip to Bayside with Howie's newly founded friends. Only Howitt could find people like these two weird locals.

Spider resembled a true representative of the Arachnid family. His short, stout body was matched to very long, spindly arms and legs. Black eyes protruded outward from his face almost as if they were on stalks able to rotate in any direction. Wispy brownish hair cascaded in all directions across his head. Anytime he opened his mouth, narrow teeth created the image of two rows of fangs. Apart from his insect-like appearance, Spider was outgoing, talkative, and hard not to laugh at.

On the other hand, Cody was nothing like his friend. The tall, skinny boy had fine features, straight black hair, close-set hazel eyes, and a way about him that almost appeared effeminate. He kept to himself, hardly ever spoke, and was certainly more reserved than his friend. The attraction for him was perhaps Spider's gregarious personality he lacked in himself.

The sun was now revealing all its brilliance as the rain front drifted out over the ocean. Vapor mists rose from the highway driven by the heat of the late afternoon solar breakthrough. Drew sat behind the front passenger side next to Cody. A few words were exchanged earlier, but now they had settled into their own thoughts. Drew stared at the passing scenery. Everything was just like the pictures in magazines and the movies. He was looking at vintage model cars of the classics: brand new, shiny Mustangs, long-finned chrome garnished Cadillacs, road burning Pontiac GTOs, and supped-up, customized Chevys of every type and year. Kids his own age were piled into convertibles, riding

Honda and Yamaha motorcycles, cut-down hot rods, and anything else having wheels. The endless stream of vehicles tooled along in both directions along the two-lane road bordering the ocean. Open stretches of marsh grass and sand dunes reached toward the water's edge on one side, while farmland sprouting an assortment of colored and multi-shaped vegetables lined the inland roadside. Small clusters and alcoves of beach houses rested between the highway and the beach, broken sporadically by the same hodgepodge collection of shops, stores, gas stations and fast food joints typical of just about anywhere along this stretch of Maryland coastline. Drew saw processions of teenagers just hanging out, walking the beach, or milling in front of the endless hamburger stands.

This is just so awesome, he thought, to be able to have friends to do all these things with. For as long as he could remember, he never had anyone his own age to do these kinds of things. What a great feeling, to be able to hang out with a bunch of guys his own age and have some fun.

Close to an hour later, a molten red sun was readying itself for its plunge into the cooling blue water stretching out toward the horizon. The air was hot and thick, heavy with its burden of solar heat and moisture sucked from a helpless ocean surface. Spider turned off the main highway and spun the boxy station wagon through a maze of narrow streets that were more like alleyways.

"Come on wild man, floor this bastard!" Roach blurted out, his words hardly wasted as Spider pushed the pedal downward and launched his passengers into the labyrinth of sand-covered, dirt roads twisting through the cottage and beach house neighborhood.

Two near collisions later, a station wagon full of screaming, laughing, and cursing male voices spun in half circle stop a in a cloud of red dust bellowing off the dirt parking lot of the Inferno nightclub.

"You UFO alien, commie bastard scared the balls right off of me!" Roach shouted, as he jumped from the passenger door. "What did you have to do to get your license? Not kill anybody during your road test?"

"He must have been taught by the same guy you learned from," Jeff added sarcastically.

"You don't understand. I know what I'm doing," Roach replied confidently. A blast of abusive obscenities followed his pretentious statement.

Within minutes of their arrival, a murky dimness began to creep across the open lot, as cars filled the parking lot in the fading evening light. The sky was a perfect mix of subtle reds on the western horizon layered on top with a deep blue merging with a navy black cover. Silhouetted against this magnificent backdrop was a huge, wooden building. The obtrusive structure had been a turn-of-the-century concert hall now converted into a sound blasting, beer drinking, rock and roll beachfront hotspot. Dark, windowed towers spiraled upward from the corners of the building, caressed on both sides by the limbs of giant pin oak trees. An enormous, continuous tube of crimson light scripted out the Inferno name easily seen from the surrounding roads or even from boats approaching the nearby docks. The rest of the building outside faded into the enveloping darkness, simply relying on its single-lighted nameplate to attract attention. Large doors were swung wide open attempting to draw in the evening air. Blaring music, light and noise poured outward enticing the anxious, entering patrons. It was undoubtedly the perfect seaside nightspot for anyone under thirty.

"This is amazing," gasped Red as he led the group of boys through the maze of cars pulling into the lot. The still air was heavy, mixed with the heat and humidity of the day, but it was the shore and something to be expected.

"Yeah, I think everyone can score tonight." Howie looked over at Spider and Cody. "Well, just about everyone."

The guys were drooling. Girls were everywhere in any imaginable size, shape, hair color, tans, freckles, in halter tops, short shorts, bare midriffs, with long slender legs, bulging chests and plunging necklines, and bodies any boy could die for. It was paradise.

"Spider, you are the man," was about all Jeff could mumble. "Where the hell did all these luscious chicks come from?"

"This is the main hangout for all the locals," Spider replied. "It's sort of the hot babe spot for girls not wanting to get hassled by vacationing one-night players."

A few of the guys laughed. "Not us, Spider," someone spoke out, "we'll treat them all like they're our sisters."

As the boys approached the waiting line, Spider suddenly added a new twist.

"Listen I need thirty bucks to get us in."

"I thought it was a two dollar cover charge?" Howie asked. "What's the deal on the thirty?"

"They serve beer in here, so you need to have proof that you're eighteen, but I got us covered. My brother's friend is that big bouncer at the door. If you just flash him any kind of ID, he'll let you go in and pretend you're the right age. He knows we're coming and we don't have proof, so I told him I would slip him thirty bucks for his trouble."

They grumbled, but the girls walking in quickly made them realize it would be a good investment. Drew threw in a five-dollar bill. Minutes later, the big bouncer, thirty

A Lasting Summer

dollars richer, slapped them on the shoulders as they walked by wishing them luck in their pursuits of female quarry.

A giant, dark, heavy wooden bar stretched almost the entire length of the sidewall directly across from an equally large stage. Shelves of liquor bottles perched behind the bar in front of a long mirror trimmed with red twinkle lights. Even though there were stools at the bar, and a few tables and chairs scattered around, the inside of the Inferno was basically an open cavern designed for a large crowd of standers and dancers. Four bartenders worked the expansive bar, serving up a multitude of drinks to the gathering crowd, but oversized glasses of beer seemed to be the mainstay. Subdued lighting positioned throughout the interior kept the expansive area in a semi-dark state. People clustered around, obviously in familiar groups. The guys were no different. They gathered together, a little intimidated by this new, alien environment.

"This bitch'n place rocks," Howie blurted out. "We are in the score column tonight, boys!"

Amazement was written over everyone's face. Drew simply thought this was another world. Guys were hanging out in packs. Girls were frittering around in groups. The whole scene was of young adults and underage teens taking in the music, dancing, and some heavy-duty drinking.

"Okay, boys, let's pound some beers," Roach announced breaking their trance.

"Keep it cool," Spider added, "and don't start acting like assholes, so we get thrown out before all the action cooks up."

"Yeah, we're cool," replied Roach, "just stay out of my way and let a real hillbilly show you boys how to pound a few beers."

Two hours later, a crowd had filled the Inferno. It wasn't exactly shoulder-to-shoulder, but there wasn't much room to maneuver. Drew had limited himself to only two glasses of beer, remindful of his drinking experience that somehow led him into this mess. Red was pacing himself close to Drew's intake, but Roach, Howie, Reegs and Jeff were more than into the fact they could drink at a bar. Enforced by an uncounted number of beers, they were laughing, joking, and making comments to just about any girl walking by. Some girls were insulted by their boisterous actions, but most were enjoying their antics. In fact, they were attracting an assortment of girls who were curious about this group of guys who didn't seem to be locals.

Drew last saw Skip, Cody and Spider about an hour ago and was wondering where they had wandered off. Constantly in his mind was the girl from the beach. He had scanned every girl that walked in, but still no sight of her. What was the chance, he reasoned, that she would even be here since Bayside was at least forty miles from Ocean Heights. Besides, she might not even be a local, but just a tourist like himself. It was past nine-thirty. Reluctantly, he was giving up on any hope he might see her tonight.

"Hey girl, we're going to have a great time tonight!"

Tori vacantly smiled at her friend's comment. Kelli had rushed her out of the house not long after she had finished working. She had spent the day hoping to see the boy from the picture, but the steady rain had kept most people away from the beach and boardwalk shops. When Kelli stopped in to visit, she had picked up on Tori's depression. She had convinced her friend a night at the Inferno might cheer her up and focus on something else.

A Lasting Summer

"I'm not sure I want to go all the way to Bayside," Tori murmured. "Besides, they serve liquor there so I'll have to borrow Katie's ID card."

"Well she won't mind, because I know she has to work to closing tonight and probably will just hang around later with her boyfriend." Kelli's older sister Katie had such similar features to Tori they sometimes were thought to be sisters.

"Okay, maybe, but you know those older guys just start hitting on us as soon as we walk in."

"What's wrong with that? I think that might brighten up your spirits. Besides we usually know most of the local guys anyhow."

"I suppose you're right, but I am worried about Jason showing up."

"I told you I would handle the creep asshole prep if he starts on you."

Tori eyes twinkled at the mere thought. "I know you will, and boy do I feel sorry for him if he were to walk in."

"Great! I'll be at you house by nine and then the party starts to cook!"

"Yeah, I am home on leave, then off to Nam to kick some slant-eye, commie ass. The Army usually gives you a week furlough after all the Special Forces training."

"You look pretty young to be a Green Beret soldier," beamed the well-tanned, shapely blond.

Roach took a gulp of beer then a pull on his cigarette. "Sure, but looks are deceiving. I've had three months of all this special jungle training and learned ten different ways to kill a gook with my bare hands. I just lost a lot of weight with all that training, so I kind of look young."

Jeff and Reegs stood off to the side doing everything possible to hold back their laughter.

"I suppose that happens," the twenty-year old girl replied bending forward to reveal more cleavage. "But, I thought all you guys had your hair cut super short."

"Oh yeah, but I was in the field so long I didn't have a chance to get it cut yet. The first sergeant is pissed at me, but I told him to kiss off."

"Cool," she purred. "You really are a hard-ass."

Drew lingered off to the side nursing a lukewarm beer. He was amused at the charade Roach was using on the girls. Most just shrugged off his idle banter and a few, like this one, were actually captivated. As goofy as it was, Drew realized that Roach, Jeff and the rest of the guys were just having a good time. It was harmless fun with no one getting hurt or upset at their adolescent bravado. His father must have been just like them. He would have never known about any of this if this unexplainable time reversal hadn't taken place. It was as if a power was interceding, bringing all this out to him. So many things were revealing themselves, but his confusion remained. Why this? Why now? And, why did it have to be some gorgeous girl he would never see again . . . .

The blood drained from his brain like a cascading waterfall. His eyes went from exploding stars of pulsating light to dull blindness. Wobbly knees were the least of his problems because he couldn't even feel them at the moment. His blurred vision framed an image in the entrance. An illusion of sorts, he weakly reasoned, but the girl from the beach was now standing there.

Fate does have its unsuspecting ways with people and events. Chance occurrences are never quite that, but rather, well-planned, charted courses for two people whose lives would never be quite the same again. Drew gasped for breath, speechless and immovable. An instant later, Tori's eyes locked on his piercing stare.

"Oh my God," she mumbled incoherently, still frozen in his sight.

"Come on, Tori, let's work our way to the stage." Kelli firmly pushed her rigid friend from behind unable to see around her taller friend. "What's the hold up? Is that piss-ant Jason in there?"

"Umm, umm . . . . ," was the best Tori could say.

"Get a grip, girl. I've never seen you act like this before."

Drew shyly looked away. He was never forward with people, and especially girls,

"Hi." Tori had made the first move determined not to let this opportunity pass. "That picture on the beach was pretty unusual."

"Yeah, unusual." He could feel his face getting redder by the minute. Drew was lost in her beauty, staring deeply into eyes he would never forget.

"Do you live around here?" she asked.

"No, I don't live here" he stammered nervously, "just sort of visiting."

"Wow, I can't believe you would end up here, especially tonight," Tori continued. "You and I just seem to keep running into each other in the most unexpected situations."

"Yeah, weird thing." Drew was sweating knowing he was making a fool of himself with the most beautiful girl he had ever talked to, in fact the only girl he had ever the courage to talk to.

"I didn't think you looked like one of the local guys."

"I'm from Columbus, Ohio," he struggled with the words. "Just down here for the week with a bunch of my friends. But, I do have an aunt that lives in Ocean Heights. Betty Ferguson."

"Oh my God, I know her and her husband Jake. They only live a few blocks from my house over on Bayside Drive."

"Hey, before we miss each other again, my name is Tori." She extended her hand warmly.

"Oh, okay," he stuttered, "nice to meet you too."

Tori smiled amusingly. "You do have a name?"

"Yeah, sure it's Drew. No, I mean Andy. Andy Michaels."

Minutes later, the main attraction of the night took to the stage. The Inferno booked throughout the summer season a number of live groups, most being newcomers trying to break into the pop music scene. Tonight was a return of one of the more popular ones, Wilbur and the Counts. Their sound was rock and roll, Motown influenced black music pounded out by a four-member band, and the lead singer, Wilbur himself. The crowd was especially large tonight because of the popularity of this band, and Wilbur played up to the cheering and blaring from his appreciative fans. A combination of beer, jammed in people, blasting music, and a lead singer gyrating on the stage had everyone dancing, singing and just having a great time.

Tori and Drew remained off to the side, as if they were the only two people in the building. They could barely talk over the blaring music, but something real and magical was beginning to happen. Their physical presence with each other was enough.

"Hey, babe, I knew you would hook up with me here tonight. This is the perfect spot to have a few beers, and maybe hang out on that nice, dark beach." A deep voice smirked.

Tori spun around enraged at the belittling remark from the all too familiar voice.

"Why don't you just get away from me, you jerk!" Tori lashed out. "You come around anytime you please thinking I have a thing for you. I want you to leave me alone."

"What's with the attitude? Are you mad at me because I wasn't around today, or are you snubbing me because I'm not some local huckster."

"You're right to everything you said, but more so because you're just a pompous ass!"

A smile broke across Drew's face underestimating the wrath and scorn that this quiet beautiful girl could unleash.

"Hey, you sand bum yokel, what the hell are you smiling at?"

"Leave him out this, Jason." Tori moved between the two boys worried about Drew and the animosity he was getting from her hated suitor. "He's just visiting his aunt and uncle in town, and I agreed to show him around and keep him company."

"Yeah, I bet you did," Jason fired back. "What's on the menu tonight, cold fish."

A fiery rage instantly welled up in Drew. He never experienced this kind of anger, especially over a girl, but the remarks weren't just directed at any girl. Tori was being mistreated by this preppy looking, conceited idiot. He tightened his fists into a ball and started moving towards Jason.

"No, Andy stay away from him! This has nothing to do with you."

Tori stood in the path of the two evenly sized boys. She could see Andy seething after the remarks both of them had received. Jason stood in his normal pompous, too good for everyone stance. A sarcastic smile etched on his face.

"Listen, Andy, he's not worth the effort," Tori said with an upset, strained tone. "He's only trying to ruin my evening and our time together."

"Listen to the bitch, whatever your name is," Jason sneered as he grabbed Tori by the arm. "She's not worth the chance of you getting your ass kicked."

An inner ferocity pushed Drew over the edge. He exploded, driving his shoulder into Jason's abdomen in a crushing tackle. His momentum carried both boys across the floor with accompanying shouts and screams. Drew found himself lying across the surprised Jason. Within seconds Jason responded with wild flaying punches and kicks trying to get off the floor and gain an advantage. A wild right caught Drew in the temple stunning him so he couldn't move. He remembered more people jumping into the melee amid shouts of "fight."

Minutes later, the combatants were in the grasp of the huge bouncers. Roach, Jeff, Red, Howie and Reegs were all there holding on to guys who appeared to be Jason's friends. The pushing, shoving, and cursing continued with the groups, but in didn't matter since they were all being escorted out of the Inferno. Drew wildly looked around, but there was no sign of Tori or her friend Kelli. Things had just happened so quickly and unexpectedly.

Jason continued shouting across the parking lot as he and his friends were being led to their cars. "I'll get you! I'll find your hick faggot ass if it's the last thing I do this summer!"

Roach held up his middle finger.

A Lasting Summer

"You too! You skinny-ass, four-eyed queer! I'm going to send all you losers home in body bags!"

Spider and Cody had somehow magically appeared with the big station wagon. Skip sat meekly in the backseat. The guys piled in and in minutes were heading back to Ocean Heights.

"Sorry I ruined the night for you guys," Drew spoke in an apologetic tone. "I know you were all having a good time."

"Don't worry about it, Andy," replied Red. "We're always there for each other."

"Hey, man, you took on the biggest dickhead in Ocean Heights." Spider said. "Jason Eastman comes down every summer with his family like they own the whole town. He's been trying to make it with Tori Randall for the past two years, but she won't have anything to do with him. She's one awesome chick!"

This last comment met with the approval of the entire car. Laughter replaced anger, and before long the talk centered at finding a place to eat.

Drew was lost in his thoughts. He just had the best evening of his life with the most perfect girl he could ever have wanted. Somehow he did the unexpected. He had fought for someone for whom he really cared. Yet, his guilt bubbled to the surface as his fight with Jason may have driven her away. Did it really matter? Drew was desperate to be with a girl who was existing thirty-five years in the past.

CHAPTER TEN

Thursday, August 11, 1965

A soft, caressing sea breeze drifted across the boardwalk. Gulls lazily rode the thermal currents rising from the warming sand. The incoming waves gently rolled over themselves as they fought the pulling tug of an outgoing tide. The scene was blissful serenity to the start of another perfect summer day.

The boy walking the boardwalk path wasn't affected by the tranquility. His night had been filled with apprehensive tossing and turning, along with fitful bouts of denial, doubt, yearning and questioning. He was more confused than he could have imagined. So much had happened in this place. Maybe it was just a dream, but the unexplainable emotions and desires seemed real. He was forming a strong connection to a time and place from some other era. More so, a bigger problem was his growing attraction to a girl he knew he would have to leave behind. Why did things have to be so right and suddenly so complicated? He never did things like this before. A fight with another boy, especially over something as ridiculous as a girl, just wasn't him. Jealousy was an emotion he had never felt, but why now?

Drew dejectedly slumped on a bench. He stared down the boardwalk toward Playland, the spot where all his troubles began.

A Lasting Summer

"I knew you would be here."

He spun around looking at a stern, serious face.

"I didn't think I would ever see you again," he responded in a bewildered voice.

"Yeah, so therefore I must be crazy talking to you now."

Drew shifted his eyes towards the ocean. "I'm sorry about last night."

"You should be." Tori continued a bit more casually. "I still don't know why I came down here before work hoping to find you."

"It probably was to tell me off."

"Probably."

"But, you're not sure?"

"No, I am not sure about anything right now," Tori sighed. "I usually never waste my time with some vacationing out-of-town boy, but there's something about you . . ."

"I promise I won't bother you anymore," Drew looked into her eyes, "if that's what you want."

She twirled around heading towards the boardwalk shops.

"You decide." A coy smile broke across her face. "Tonight, seven-thirty, right here."

"Oh my, God, she's still interested in me." Drew shook his head in disbelief as she walked away. "What am I doing with such an unbelievable girl?"

It seemed like an eternity away before he would meet up with Tori. Drew had spent time on the beach with the guys lying around and just hanging out. It was fun and something that Drew was learning to appreciate even more, but his mind was a million miles away. He couldn't believe that Tori wanted to see him again. Things like this just never happened to him. Most of the girls from school paid little attention to him, but Tori was different. She seemed to be bringing something out of him. He was starting to feel wanted. Yet, in another two days they would all be heading home.

A painful thought suddenly clouded his thinking. What was back home? Would his life he left last week still be there? Maybe the old fisherman was an angel or a ghost, and Drew had actually died. As bad as this sounded, something more profound was beginning to envelope him. What would happen to Tori? This wasn't something he had bargained for. He thought of her all the time. Maybe it was because she was the first girl interested in him, but he quickly dismissed this thought. Tori was much more. What would happen with her after Sunday?

Drew needed some answers and he needed them fast. He told the guys that he was starting to get sunburned and he was heading back to the cottage. None of the other guys offered to go with him, so he had nothing to stop him from going right to the one person that might be able to give him some answers.

"Madam Zahrah, are you here?"

He stood in the middle of the shop. Despite the brightness outside, the interior was again cast in a shadowing darkness. Drew patiently waited for a response. As the back curtain separated, his disappointment matched the surroundings.

"Hi Andy. I didn't expect you back."

"I was hoping I could find some answers," he said.

Jonne had a paint-splattered apron draped from her neck with her hair tucked under a baseball cap. Despite her messy clothing she was still a stunning beauty.

"You look disappointed to see me," she began. "You always seem to catch me looking my worse."

"No, Jonne, I am glad to see you, but I was hoping Madam Zahrah would be here. Is she out to lunch, or something?"

"Sorry again, Andy, but she's sick and won't be in today. I was just painting some chairs to put around the table."

Drew was feeling the rising frustration of the past few days. Every time he thought he might have some explanation for his predicament, another dead end appeared. He was running out of hope.

"I know you must be disappointed, but do you really need Madam Zahrah's advice that badly?"

"You wouldn't believe me one bit if I told you how desperate I am."

Jonne motioned to the chairs around the table in the same spot as the previous day. They seemed untouched from the way he remembered them.

"I might not be who you are looking for, but I'm a pretty good listener," Jonne said.

Surprisingly, Drew felt comfortable with this girl. She was friendly and was willing to talk to him, so he sat down and began telling his story. Besides, who else could he turn to now?

Twenty minutes later, Jonne shook her head. She hadn't laughed and never interrupted him during his story of his encounters in Ocean Heights. He just knew that she thought he was crazy.

"Wow!" She took her baseball cap off and shook out the long strands of black, silky hair.

"I figured you wouldn't believe me." Drew lowered his eyes embarrassed with the incredible story. "I just thought Madam Zahrah might know about these kinds of things."

"Actually, I think your situation might be out of her league."

Drew rose from the chair.

"Sit down," the girl ordered in a pleasant, but firm tone.

"Andy, or Drew," she proceeded, "there definitely are forces working here that are more powerful than anyone can explain. The legends of the shore are endless, but people over the years have described these strange occurrences, both good and bad, that have happened."

"Do you think there are bad things and people doing this to me?" he questioned.

"I don't think so. I believe there are forces and people out there trying to help you."

"With what?" Drew was wondering how his placement in a different time and with total strangers could ever be helping him.

"Andy, you grew up without ever knowing your father. Maybe this is a chance to learn what he was like, and what his life like was through your own eyes. You needed to become him to become you."

"I don't understand what you mean by that," said Drew. "I know what I want. I want to graduate and just go away and start my own life."

"Can you?" Jonne stared hard with her piercing eyes.

"I am not sure."

"That's what I mean," she continued. "To me, your heart is frozen in confusion and despair because of what you never had—a father to grow up with."

The truth might set one free, but Drew was not willing to accept the words of a total stranger, regardless if Jonne was a person trying to help him.

"I have to go." Drew pushed the chair back annoyed at things he didn't want to hear. "What about this fisherman, who is this guy?"

"He might reveal himself again," said Jonne, "but the spirits that dwell on the shore choose their own time to bid their explanation. You may never see him again."

That was the last thing Drew needed to hear.

"One more thing, Jonne." He paused because the question he was about to ask her might be the most painful. "What will happen with Tori and me?"

Jonne smiled warmly. "Fortunately, or perhaps unfortunately, Destiny has entered into your situation. No one can say what her part will be, but enjoy every minute you have with her. Remember, your life is back home in Columbus in another time."

"Hi, Andy." Tori's voice broke his thinking. "Guess you accepted my invitation."

He hadn't seen her approaching through the throng of people starting to crowd the boardwalk. Drew smiled at the sight he had waited all day for, however his mind was twisting after his talk with Jonne. She had said things to him that were true, yet he never wanted to admit. She couldn't explain what was going on, but what did she know anyhow? She sure wasn't a reader of fortunes or savior of the lost. She was just some cleaning girl. Nevertheless, her most disturbing remarks had been about Tori. She was all that mattered to him now.

"Thanks for giving me another chance." Drew stumbled for the next few words. "I think you're the best thing that's happened to me since I arrived."

Tori blushed unable to reply. This was so much not her style. She was acting like some flighty freshman girl.

"Did you get a chance to eat?" She asked regaining some composure.

"Not really."

"Well," said Tori, "let's head to Thrasher's."

They engaged in idle conversation as they moved along with the flow of tourists. The temperatures began to slide into the low eighties; a welcome relief from the day's blistering heat. With a pleasant land breeze and the sun setting off to the west, it was a beautiful evening to be on the boardwalk. Drew was adjusting to the shore and his new time frame. Tori was the perfect companion and distraction. It was amazing that he was able to talk to her about so many things despite the fact they were from different eras.

A short time later, they reached their destination. Thrasher's turned out to be an open-stand, burger joint on the corner of the boardwalk and St. Louis Avenue. Drew didn't know what the attraction was because a line of at least ten people waited patiently for something from the restaurant. Whatever it was, it smelled pretty good.

"Best French fries on the boardwalk," Tori said, "and probably the best along the whole Atlantic coast."

"All this waiting for French fries?" asked Drew.

"Just you wait and see."

Fifteen minutes later, Drew was trying to manage an overflowing, oversized cup of French fries. They looked incredible.

"Okay, now you don't want to look totally like a tourist," Tori laughed, "so don't ask for ketchup. You can only eat them with salt and plenty of vinegar."

"You have to be kidding." Drew wasn't much the person to try new types of foods or combinations, but this girl could convince him of just about anything.

"Unbelievable!" Drew had never tasted anything so different, and so good.

"That was my reaction when I first had one," added Tori.

"How long have you lived here?"

"A little over three years."

"All this time I thought you were a local, born and raised here."

"Not quite, but then again I am not a tourist like someone I know," she responded with a playful swipe at his shoulder. "I have lived here long enough to qualify as a true local. I've seen Lady Francine."

Drew looked puzzled. "Who is she? The mayor of the town?"

"Don't be funny," she chided, "She's the ghost of the boardwalk."

"Yeah, sure. More of these hocus pocus legends that I keep hearing about."

"I thought the same way, but about a year ago I spotted her strolling on the boardwalk in her funny clothes. She stopped and waved at me, and before I could say anything, she was gone. She just vanished."

Before Drew could ask another question, Tori was dragging him towards a soda stand specializing in cherry cokes.

"So, what are you going to do after you graduate from high school this year?" asked Tori as she sipped her cherry coke.

"I think I want to go to college, but if anything at all, just get away from home."

Tori picked up some animosity in Drew's tone.

"What about you? Staying here in Ocean Heights?"

"I love it here, but I don't think it will be for very much longer." A sad look clouded her eyes. "My father was stationed here three years ago. About a month ago he told us that we will probably be moving by spring."

She noticed Drew's confused look. "He's in the Navy and probably will be assigned to San Diego. You know, with the war escalating."

"Yeah, I know it gets pretty intense from things I learned in history class."

Tori was a bit puzzled by Drew's future reference to the Vietnam war.

"Anyway, this has been the best assignment station for me and my sister. Kelli is the closest friend I ever have had, and I just love being near the ocean and boardwalk. But, being a Navy brat keeps you moving around."

"How does your mother feel about moving?"

A deeper sadness crept over Tori's beautiful face. "She died of cancer about seven years ago. She never cared for Navy life. Just too many moves for her."

Drew decided to not pursue the topic any further. With his similar situation he had so much to share with her, but this was the wrong time.

"Hey, Andy, let's head toward Playland." Tori picked up spirits and her enthusiasm. "There's plenty to do and maybe we'll see Kelli there."

Their walk continued down the wooden boulevard. Past an assortment of food stands lining the path: Candy Kitchen Old Fashion Taffy, Dumser's Dairyland, Fisher's popcorn, Kohr Brother's frozen custard, The Nut House, Shelly's Soft Shell Crab Shack, Sneaky Pete's sub shop, and Boog's Barbeuce. Tori kept him amused with a running history of their origin and well-known culinary specialties. If it wasn't food stands, it was the collection of unusual shops catching Drew's attention. The Ocean Gallery had an eclectic display of original oil paintings capturing every imaginable interest of gawking sightseers. Ripley's Believe It Or Not Museum had a twenty foot replica of a great white shark crashing through its side wall and out through the slopping roof. Moondoggie's Surf Shop was surrounded by Jack the Ripper's Wax Museum on one side, and Madam Cleo's Palm Reading Palace on the other. The sights were endless, but all of them captivated Drew and certainly his guide.

Playland was in full regalia of lights, sounds, smells, banner, flags, and posters—anything to draw in patrons to its many offerings. For Drew it was a whirlwind night as Tori led him from the Pharaoh's Fury swinging galley ship, to the Tidal Wave, the Hurricane, the Tornado, and a creaky, scary wooden roller coaster called the Comet. She persuaded him to walk through the Magic Carpet Haunted House, and rushed him indoors to ride Bumper Cars and mini boats floating in an indoor pool. Somewhere in between his busy night, Tori introduced him to Kelli as they ran into her and some other local girls.

"Come on, Andy, we have a few more rides."

Her energy was contagious, as Drew couldn't resist her charm and her persuasion. High on top the Giant Ferris Wheel, he looked down the glowing strip of the boardwalk edged against a black ocean. He wondered if the fisherman was out tonight and if he would ever see him again. Next, she led him to the Venetian Carousel where he rode a brightly painted smiling camel. Tori was perched on a charging white stallion, and she never looked more beautiful.

Leaving the midway, they were walking past a funny looking booth when she grabbed his arm. "Oh, we have to do this," she giggled.

They squeezed close together inside the phone-size booth. Tori drew a black curtain across the doorway, and then slipped in a quarter into the metal slot. Seconds later, a red light appeared followed by a whirring sound, and then the flash of a light bulb. The process was repeated three more times. They waited a few minutes outside the booth when a strip of four black and white photos trailed out of a chute. Four different pictures captured poses of Tori and him hamming it up for the camera.

Close to midnight, the lights along the strip began to extinguish one by one as the crowds drifted away and tired vendors closed down for the night. They had wandered to a small alcove that jutted off the boardwalk with a perfect view of the ocean. Stars seemed to bounce their rays off the tops of the rolling waves illuminating them in an effervescent sparkle. The two newly found friends sat in silence enjoying the magic of the night and the chemistry of each other.

"Thanks again for the great time tonight and for giving me another chance," Drew quietly spoke.

"You are very welcome, but we might want to thank that reporter guy for putting us in that picture." Her expression was total sincerity. "If he hadn't been there, then we wouldn't be here right now. It's all destiny you know."

Drew grimaced. All this fate and destiny stuff seemed to be leading him around, but this journey was turning into more. Tori was beyond belief.

"I liked your friend, Kelli."

"Thanks, and I think all your friends are sort of interesting, but very nice."

They both laughed in unison.

"Well, Andy, time to head home before I get into to a jam with my dad. He's pretty cool about things, but I still have that midnight summer curfew."

"Should I walk you home?" he asked naively.

She giggled at his shyness. "That would be nice, but how about just to the end of my street so your friends don't get the wrong impression."

A Lasting Summer

A few minutes later Drew was standing in the murky light of an ancient streetlight. Tori was inches from him. He was completely bewildered.

"Hey thanks for the evening. You made me a believer. There are still a few decent boys still out there."

She reached up and placed a quick kiss on his lips.

Drew was speechless and paralyzed.

"I am off all day tomorrow, so maybe we can meet on the beach if you want." Tori offered the invitation as she slipped into the shadows of tree-lined sidewalk.

"Okay," he replied not quite sure how to react.

"Just look near the pavilion around ten-thirty. See you then."

She was gone. Drew stared at the lifeless street.

"What is going on?" he thought. "Things like this never happen to me."

CHAPTER ELEVEN

Friday, August 12, 1965

The Harbor Point Hotel was one of those majestic old structures, one growing more elegant and stately over time. Massive pillars supported five floors and well over fifty rooms. A continuous walkway wrapped around each floor with expansive porches at each end. Nestled at the south end of Ocean Heights and set back from the beach, it was built over a hundred years ago. Attracting a large number of the wealthy and prosperous from Boston, these affluent vacationers wanted to be far from the smelly fishing shacks, unsightly piers, and hodge-podge cottages along the ocean shore. In doing so, an undeveloped tract of land overlooking Southport Bay on the opposite side of the Ocean Heights proper was selected. Unfortunately, building on this location destroyed vast acres of salt marsh, mud flats, and tidal pools. Little issue was voiced over the destruction of nesting sites of the countless species of birds inhabiting the marshy areas. Along with this, it disrupted the normal tide and current flows eventually affecting the myriad of marine invertebrates living in the pools and muddy banks of the bay. It just didn't matter back then. These were well before the days of environmental awareness and stewardship. As with so many other areas in the country of unspoiled natural beauty, money and power paved the way.

A Lasting Summer

Jason Baxter Mahoney sipped his freshly squeezed orange juice in the comfort of the Trade Winds Cabana on the covered terrace of the Harbor Point Hotel. His family leased the fifth floor governor's suite for most of the summer and he could dine in any of the four restaurants in the hotel. He was in a sullen mood. Sitting under his glass of orange juice was an undergrad catalog for Harvard. Being fourth generation, it was just assumed he would be heading to the prestigious college after his senior year at Yarlington Prep School. At the moment, he was showing more interest in a sales brochure for a new car. He was tired of the Mustang and was considering one of those German-made sports cars. A Porsche was what a Yarlington classmate owned. He was pissed that this car had blown his Mustang away in a race on Lexington Boulevard.

Despite the classic lines of the sports cars and females adorning the brochure, Jason was bored. His third year down here and four weeks into the summer, he was finding little to hold his interest. Girls were easy to pick up. Spend a little time with them and you got whatever you wanted. There was no challenge. The vacationing girls were twits and the locals weren't worth a second look, all except for one.

"Hey, Jason, I've been looking around this dump for you."

He looked up from his reading. "Pretty early for you, Evan. I thought you didn't rise much before noon."

"No, I usually don't, but I needed to find you," Evan smirked. His bleached hair was a tangle of strands. Deep set eyes and a narrow face covered in freckles projected his mischievous nature.

"So, what's the deal?"

"I didn't see you on the boardwalk last night."

"That's right," Jason yawned. "I was busy elsewhere."

"Another big score, I guess."

"If you call Mona being on the scoring sheet, then I forfeit my points for last night."

Both boys laughed mockingly.

"Well," continued Evan, "last night I was cruising the scene when guess who came walking out of the Magic Carpet at Playland. None other than your most desired wish, Tori Randall."

Jason immediately sat up, tossing the brochure on the table.

"Man, she looked hot enough to melt paint off the walls."

"Don't screw with me," Jason replied angrily.

"I'm not lying. But, there's more to the story."

"Was she with that bitch friend of hers?"

Evan twisted his face into a vengeful snarl.

"She was hanging out with that loser from The Inferno; the guy you went at it with."

Jason jumped up knocking chairs over and quickly drawing the attention of the other patrons seated at breakfast.

"I knew he was moving in on her!" Jason burst out, spit flying from his mouth as his anger intensified. It was bad enough to have Tori be with another guy, but this guy . . . .

"I followed them down the boardwalk and I'll tell you, it looked liked she was having a great time with him." Evan snickered, knowing quite well what he was instigating.

The shorter boy suddenly found himself on his toes as Jason grabbed him by the front of the shirt. "Why didn't you come and get me."

"We tried to find you, James and I, but we didn't know where you went with the chick," Evan gasped as his shirt tightened around his neck.

Jason violently shoved him away. He was in a total rage.

"I want his ass!"

"Maybe if we cruise the boardwalk tonight we can find him."

"I'm not waiting for tonight," Jason shouted. "He'll be somewhere on the beach or boardwalk today with his loser friends."

"Okay, okay. I'll call James and maybe he can get some of the Dover guys to hook up with us."

"Now, right now!!" Jason jumped up, out of control and out of his mind.

"Would you please hurry up!"

"I can't believe you're so impatient. Have a big date or something?"

"You can be such a pain. You're so lucky I'm your best friend."

Kelli playfully tossed a folded towel at the other girl. "Okay, Tori. I know he's like an unbelievable hunk, but get a grip here girl. He's a guy you just met."

"Sure." Tori was less than convincing. "Sure"

The morning sun was high in the sky nearing its apex. Tori wanted to be on the beach by eleven, but Kelli didn't finish her summer school class until eleven fifteen. It was a miracle she had even gone to class with the prospect of spending a day on the beach with her friend. Tori had insisted she go to school first. Nearly noon, they had just parked the car and were making their way to the beach.

"Come on, Tori, what's the deal?" asked Kelli stopping on the boardwalk.

Tori was restless and more apprehensive than usual. "I'm not sure about anything. Every time I'm with him I just want to stay with him. I can't describe what's happening to me."

"We talked about that already, Tori, but there's something else, isn't there?"

Tori hesitated looking for the right words. "I know people say you can't fall in love at first sight, but he's just so good to be with." She hesitated, but knowing what she had to say. "Kelli, I don't want this to ever end."

"Why does it have to?" her friend spoke out. "You only have one more year of high school and maybe you two can somehow work it out where you go to the same college."

"Oh, that would be great!" Tori momentarily beamed, but she knew in her heart things like this never prove true as they do in fairy tales.

They moved off the boardwalk down wooden steps shedding their sandals as they started walking across the sand. The beach was a maze of spread blankets, towels, chairs, straw mats, errant balls of every shape and size, and of course, all of humanity. Temperatures were already in the low eighties and the sun blazed through a cloudless sky. Heat waves shimmered off the sand creating distant mirages of pools of water. Nevertheless, as far as the eye could see, people of all ages romped, trudged, ran, strolled, or simply lay in the basking cauldron of sun, sand and water.

"Hey, Tori, over here!"

She spun her head toward the familiar voice. Tori waved, smiling openly and warmly. Her day was ready to begin.

"I was wondering if I had the wrong place on the beach," Drew shyly said.

A Lasting Summer

"Kelli just took forever."

"Why do you always blame me?" Kelli tried to defend her lack of punctuality.

Tori gave Drew a hug in full view of her friend, Red, Roach, and the rest of the guys. It didn't matter to her because it just felt so right.

Howie shook his head in disbelief. Andy always seemed to attract the best looking girls, but this one was beyond anything he could imagine. Not only was she gorgeous, she also had a great personality and was fun to be around. She wasn't a miserable princess like so many girls he was encountering. Well, she did bring her friend who was pretty decent looking and there was always that possibility.

The guys jockeyed their towels and blankets around giving the girls any spot they wanted. Once they were all rearranged they began talking about the boardwalk and beach scene in Ocean Heights. Tori and Drew moved closer to each other wishing they could be the only two people on the beach. Privacy wasn't a possibility, yet they were still having a great time with all their friends.

Not much later, Cody and Spider unexpectedly arrived. Dressed in pants and long sleeve shirts, they seemed hardly ready for a day at the beach. They seemed to be winded and appeared visibly flustered.

"Hey, guys." Spider tried to settle his breathing. "We're glad we found all of you together."

"What's wrong?" asked Kelli detecting their agitation.

"Jason and his frat buddies are looking all over for you, especially Tori and Andy," Spider reluctantly announced. "Some of the carneys at the arcade told me that Jason is cruising the boardwalk because he thinks you'll be showing up for work. What he really wants is a piece of Andy and any of his friends."

Tori nervously shrugged her shoulders. "I guess it's a good thing I'm off today,"

"Yeah, but it's only going to be a matter of time before they start searching the beach," Kelli added. "We have to get out of here."

"I'm not running away from any commie fags," Roach blurted out jumping to his feet and poised for a fight. "We'll give those preppies everything they can handle."

"No, you can't cause any trouble," Kelli quickly responded, "because the beach patrol or lifeguards will kick you off the beach for the rest of the day and sometimes for the whole week."

"She's right," Tori said. "We can't stay here."

Drew was getting more depressed by the minute thinking his impulsiveness may have brought all this trouble to Tori, Kelli and all the guys.

"Hey, we might have a solution." Spider seemed confident in his tone. "Why don't we clear out of here and just head up to the North End."

"Great idea!" Kelli agreed openly. "Those idiots probably don't even know that it exists. Let's pack up and get out of here."

Minutes later, their entourage was moving through the maze of beach umbrellas keeping them well out of sight from anyone trying to spot them from the boardwalk. Cody and Spider knew a shortcut to their parked station wagon, getting them off the main thoroughfare as quickly as possible.

Drew kept close to Tori. His perfect day had been unexpectedly thrown into turmoil.

"You'll like the North End." Tori placed her hand into his. He jumped at first contact, but he knew he didn't want to let go. Her energy flowed into his body awakening every

A Lasting Summer

nerve and sensation. "It's very isolated and quiet. That's why only the locals know about it."

Drew held her hand tightly. "Tori, I would follow you to the ends of the earth to be with you." She smiled knowing it was true. She felt the same way.

The north end of Ocean Heights was an area known only to the locals. Sitting four miles out of town, it was their private getaway from the roving bands of tourists and sunbathers. Not that they didn't enjoy the influx of vacationers and the money they brought into the local economy. It was simply an escape from the commotion and a place where the citizens of Ocean Heights could relax on the Maryland shore.

Rocky Point Lighthouse Park was a subtle side note on all the tourist guides. Any mention of rocks sent vacationers running since they didn't travel all this way to stroll or swim on a rocky beach. The founding fathers of Ocean Heights must have correctly guessed future events for their beachfront community the name kept everyone away except for the locals. Most anyone would have been shocked to see the real Rocky Point. It jutted out from the surrounding treed park and down a five-foot bank, a flat beach with almost pure white sand stretched in either direction, with an occasional dead tree, twisted skeleton limbs and a splintered, ravished trunk lay in contorted repose near the higher sand dunes. A likely victim of the '62 hurricane, it was testimony to the savage power of a storm driven ocean. The sparkling sand was littered only with the tiny remains of countless empty shells from lifeless crustaceans and mollusks. If undisturbed, fiddler crabs scurried from their sandy burrows through the endless tidal pools searching for bits of detritus. Gulls, sandpipers, and a vast assortment of marine birds soared along the ocean breezes and currents of rising air. It was a majestic scene of unspoiled nature, and the best part was that only a few humans walked or sat along this incredible paradise.

Spider wheeled the bulky station wagon off the paved highway onto a sandy dirt road hardly visible to the unnoticing. Kelli followed closely behind with Tori and Drew squeezed into her VW bug. The road twisted and turned through the southern oaks, pines and underbrush forming a natural barrier to the ocean. Minutes later, Spider pulled into a town park carved out from the vegetation and nestled under shadowing trees. Situated with shelters, picnic tables, stone fireplaces, and even a brick rest room facility, the small park appeared empty. The guys piled out of the station wagon, grabbing their hastily gathered beach wear. Kelli led the way and moments later they were standing on an endless beach. They were the only ones there.

"This is incredible," Red spoke out. "Just miles of perfect, empty beach."

"Yeah, real great if you're trying to hook up with some chicks," Howie mumbled, perturbed at the lack of any possible conquests.

"Don't worry, guys," said Kelli. "I saw Jena just before we left the boardwalk. She's bringing a bunch of her friends here later for a little cookout. They're going to bring hot dogs, hamburgers, crab cakes, soda, and everything else. Our treat to you, since you guys are pretty cool and all us locals aren't that bad."

"Hey, Kelli," Roach added. "If they look anything like you and Tori, this will be a California-girl dream."

"Why is she bringing some mountain women for you," snickered Howie.

A Lasting Summer

"Maybe, but you won't have any problem finding some beached whales for yourself."

"Are you guys always this nice to each other?" Kelli shook her head in disbelief.

"Yeah, they're actually kissing cousins," said Jeff.

"But they don't French, at least not in public." Regger jumped into the mix.

This brought an onslaught of verbal abuse among all the guys. Even Drew threw a few good-natured barbs at his newly found friends. Tori and Kelli stepped back not wanting to disrupt all this so-called fun. They both actually found the guys to be quite nice and very funny. Tori, of course, saw so much more in a very special one. His laugh, his sparkling eyes, the shy voice, his tender nature, she thought. How could she not want to be with him forever.

The late afternoon sun was beginning to cast shadows. Jena had arrived earlier with six other girls and they had spent the day on the beach with Cody, Spider, and the boys. It turned out to be a great time with everyone talking, swimming, and just hanging out together. The girls brought plenty of food and the boys had gathered wood to burn in the fireplaces for cooking. A delicious meal was shared and the conversation hardly diminished as the teenagers from different parts of the country talked about their lives.

With each passing minute, the sun was sliding deeper into the western horizon, but it was departing in a bursting pallet of red, orange, yellow and gold. There was little left to the imagination, as the solar departure was equal to any summer fireworks show. The locals said a day at Rocky Point wouldn't be complete if they didn't have a fire on the beach at night. Earlier, the boys had piled up wood and before long a fire blazed in a make shift pit dug in the sand.

A shroud of darkness nibbled at the friends gathered around the fire pit, but the enveloping blackness was kept at bay by the energy of the burning wood.

Tori sat next to Drew. She had such amazing, deep-seated feelings for this boy she had just met. It was remarkable, impossible. Yet, a hurtful pain began to form in her heart. She had tried to deny all of this, simply to ignore the emotions she was beginning to feel for him. If only she could manage to accept meeting him as a wonderful summer chance, a newfound friend, it would be so easy. Perhaps, the pain tearing her apart, clouding this perfect moment would be missing from her thoughts.

"Hey, do you guys know any good ghost stories from back home?" asked Jena. Most of the group had paired off. Jena was sitting next to Jeff.

"Okay, I have one," Jeff began. "There's a story about this girl who is killed in a car accident on the way to her prom. Soon after that, people reported seeing a girl hitchhiking alongside the same road at night with her hair all done up and with a prom dress on. The scary part is some people have picked her up. She will get into the back seat of their car and give directions to get to her school because she is late for her prom. But, when the driver gets there, the girl is gone from the back of the car. Some flowers from her corsage are scattered on the seat."

Shrieks of fright and laughter exploded from the gathering. Drew spoke up. "I would like to know the story about this Lady Francine."

"It's not a story," Kelli said before any of the locals could tell their version. "She really is a spirit who lives on the boardwalk."

"What commie, lame propaganda hoax is this." Roach disgustedly flicked his cigarette into the fire.

"No, no," Kelli argued. "She really does exist. Probably everyone who has ever lived in Ocean Heights has seen her at some point." All the locals, including Tori, agreed.

"She appears in all types of clothing and in all different characters. She will be in a form she wants you to see her." Kelli continued. "Lady Francine was one of the most wealthy, prominent, beautiful women who ever lived in Ocean Heights back in the 1800's."

The boys laughed and joked about seeing someone almost a hundred and fifty years old. Drew was not ready to argue with any legend or scientifically impossible event. How could he when he was living in one at this very instant.

"The best legend is probably the one about the Captain." The normally silent Cody spoke out. "The story is about an old man who appears dressed as a fisherman coming in from the ocean out of a fog bank."

A cold rivulet of sweat ran down Drew's back.

"Well, it's sort of true because there was this sea captain who lived a long time ago in Ocean Heights, but he wasn't a fisherman. He was a member of the Life-Saving Service."

"I never heard of those guys before," one of the local girls said.

"Not many people have," Cody continued. "They were formed in 1875 to help and assist shipwreck victims all along the Delmarva Peninsula. They were the guys who went out on the ocean to rescue people. Most of the time it was during terrific storms and pounding seas."

"How do you know so much about this?" Red asked.

"My grandfather was an officer in the Coast Guard and he told me stories about its history. This Life-Saving Service operated all along this coast and even had a station in Ocean Heights. There was a lighthouse right here, so now you know why the park was given the name. The Life-Saving Service disbanded in 1914 because it was merged with the Revenue Cutters Service to form the U.S. Coast Guard.

This captain was the keeper of the Ocean Heights station. He had been on countless rescues and he was said to be the most brave and fearless of any of the Surfmen. Around 1897 off of Pope's Island, a huge Northeaster struck the Peninsula. All along the coast, Life-Savers were hauling in shipwrecked sailors. The Captain had already been involved in two rescue missions that day. He volunteered for a third rescue that everyone said would be impossible to reach. Despite the warnings, he went out on the rescue mission, but never returned. He lost his life to save three sailors who did make it to shore. They said the Captain gave up his spot on the rescue boat when they were just about to capsize because of the huge waves and water pouring into the boat."

"Wow, I never heard this story before and I've lived here all my life," Kelli shared her astonishment with the rest.

Cody glanced at her. "Maybe now you know how the pier got its name."

"Oh, my God," said Kelli, "Reader's Pier."

"Named in memory of Captain Paulson Reader," Cody nodded.

Drew was in a trance. Everything Cody had relayed in the story was coinciding with his encounter with the mysterious fisherman. He thought about the mist unexpectedly drifting in off a calm, clear sea. The figure emerging from the fog dressed in old-fashion clothing. But more so, the stranger knew Drew's name. Could it be possible he had met Captain Reader?

"Why does he mysteriously appear?" asked Red.

A Lasting Summer

"No one really knows for sure," Cody mentioned, "but he seems to come in to help people. Not from drowning or things like that, but with things messing up their lives. He comes in to guide people through their problems."

Drew's head was spinning. Did Captain Reader appear to help him find friends? He never experienced the friendships and bonds he had formed these past few days with the guys. But maybe the Captain was there to direct him to Tori. His heart sank in despair. The old man hadn't solved any of his problems, but only seemed to add to them. In one more day, Drew would be returning home, leaving Ocean Heights and Tori only in his thoughts.

"Hey, enough of this sad talk." Tori's magical smile pulled him from his frustration. She reached for his hand. "Let's go for a walk and I'll show you where the lighthouse used to be."

The couple melted into the surrounding darkness beset with a multitude of kidding remarks and suggestions. It didn't really matter to either one of them because they both wanted to be alone with each other. They walked silently, drifting casually across the hard packed sand. The tide stretched out to its furthest point in a tug-of-war with its nightly lunar opponent. With the low water, the beach appeared almost endless. The ocean was a mirror, breaking into tiny bursts of diamond moonlight dancing in rhythm to the occasional lazy rolling wave. Words weren't necessary as the teenagers walked hand in hand, dreaming of a time when they would always be together.

Their steps had led them further along the north end of the park. Drew could faintly make out the island curving around and forming another inlet to Southport Bay. The further they went he could see more of the beach disappearing into a massive, jagged outline. The noise of waves gently breaking against some object was growing stronger. Thirty feet later he was staring at the massive boulder outcrop of Rocky Point.

"A lighthouse used to be here, back there, off the beach," Tori said pointing toward the gloomy tree line, "but a hurricane destroyed most of it a long time ago. They never rebuilt it once the south inlet was dredged out to handle the bigger modern freighters heading toward the inland ports."

"Looks pretty narrow through here." Drew squinted his eyes trying to see across the open inlet.

"Lots of wrecks of those old sailing ships, and plenty of fishing trawlers along with them."

"Probably kept guys like Captain Reader pretty busy."

Tori sighed. "Can you imagine what type of person would go out in a storm to rescue perfect strangers and then sacrifice his own life so someone else could live?"

Drew thought about what Tori said. It was indeed a special type of individual who knew the risks and what the consequences might be, but still went ahead anyway to save another person. Was it their fortitude, or simply doing a job?

"I can't imagine their courage let alone their kindness and devotion to help others."

"Yeah, they were special people," Drew nodded.

"Andy, you're like them. You just make me feel so special with everything you do. You're the kindest and most gentle boy I have ever known."

Drew was startled by her words. No one had ever spoken to him like this.

Tori led them toward a large flat boulder close to the water's edge. As they both sat down, she moved as close to him as she could. Knowing how shy he might act, she made the first move. She draped his arm around her shoulders.

"I'm not sure how to tell you this," she began, "but I have never felt this way about a boy before."

Drew was perspiring, his palms were dripping, but his mouth felt as dry as the Sahara Desert.

She turned to face him.

"I know we live so far from each other, but we can stay in contact through the year. Maybe after we finish high school we could both go to the same college. Who knows, we might stay together until we can be with each other forever."

Tori was shocked at what she had just said. She was so embarrassed and was thankful the darkness hid her blushing face.

"Wouldn't it be nice." Drew barely whispered the words.

She was a bit confused by his reaction.

Drew stumbled. "To live together . . . in the kind of world . . . where we belong."

"What are you saying?"

"The words to the Beach Boys song, *Wouldn't It Be Nice*."

"Oh, my God, that's one of my favorite songs and it is perfect."

Within a millisecond, Tori reached up and kissed him. Drew's heart stopped, his blood congealed, his muscles went limp, and his brain erupted into an array of neurological explosions.

"I'm sorry for being so forward," Tori slipped into her own whisper mode. "I've never been this way with anyone."

"No, I mean, yeah, but, but . . . I mean." Drew stopped. He realized he was incoherent.

Their kisses were short, but they lasted forever. Neither wanted to leave, but they knew what their friends would be thinking.

Still out of the light of the fire, Tori stopped and wrapped her arms around Drew's neck. She knew what was next.

"Andy, I never want you to leave. I can't explain a thing, but I do know this for sure." Tori paused for a lifetime. "I love you."

What's the proper way to describe that first admission of love from someone else? That first love in your life when you're sixteen years old and you have your whole life ahead of you. Yet, you know beyond any explanation, this person is your first and everlasting love. There might be others later on, but no one else will ever capture your first true love. No, one can never forget.

He didn't respond. His world would never be the same from this moment on.

"Come on." She gently pulled his hand. "We have to leave the park soon."

Minutes later, the fire was put out, the cars loaded up, and goodbyes exchanged among the group. Obviously, the night had been a tremendous success, since everyone was talking and hugging each other.

"Hey, I only work to two o'clock tomorrow, so maybe we can hang out together for the rest of the day." Tori smiled as she held his hands. "I hope you don't think I'm some psycho freak."

"I think you unbelievable." His words were shaky and faltering.

"Yeah, sure."

A Lasting Summer

Tori got into Kelli's VW Bug and pulled out of the parking area. He stood there staring at the taillights fading down the twisting road.

"I think you're in deep trouble this time. This girl has really got your number." Red was standing behind Drew then gently put his hand on his shoulder. "Come on Andy, time to head back."

The Stratocrusier rolled out on the highway from the dirt road to Rocky Point. A catchy Beatles tune was blasting out of the radio from an AM station, WABC, out of New York City. Just about everyone inside was hollering out the lyrics and singing as out of tune as could be possible, but having a kick ass good time. On a long isolated stretch of the highway, Spider's headlights caught a shiny object on the shoulder of the road. Closer, it appeared to everyone in the car to be a person in some type of garment standing there.

"It's the ghost of the girl killed on her prom night!" Howie screamed from the back seat. "Don't stop, don't stop!"

A deathly silence filled the entire car as someone turned off the radio. The distance closed as everyone held his breath in terror. Ten feet away, the image of a young, black man dressed in the shiny material of a basketball uniform casually waved at them as they sped by. Almost in unison, everyone in the car started breathing again.

"I told you hippies it was just some guy walking!" Roach bellowed.

The entire car erupted in nervous laughter, cursing, and swearing.

Drew sat in the back of the station wagon, looking out the rear window, completely oblivious to everything. Unexpectedly, a ghost of a sea captain, his father's friends, and his father's past had all entered his life. More incredibly, a girl of his every dream, from the furthest part of his imagination, had just admitted her love to him. In one more day, he would be returning home. He would be going back to his familiar life. He twitched nervously. Something was wrong. Drew reached deep inside to realize he didn't want to go back.

CHAPTER TWELVE

Saturday, August 13, 1965

"Go in peace."

He made the sign of the cross as the priest spoke the words ending the mass. He rose from the hard kneelers and genuflected at the end of the wooden pew. As he walked through the foyer he dipped his fingers into the bowl of holy water and again blessed himself in the traditional manner. He had attended Mass every morning since arriving in Ocean Heights. The 7:45 Mass at St. Anne's Catholic Church had been early enough before anyone woke up and started to wonder where he was. It probably wouldn't have mattered, since none of the guys really cared about him. He had found a tremendous comfort in being able to attend daily Mass. Not only was he fulfilling his mother's wishes, he was doing this for himself and his own peace of mind.

Skip had grown up with the guys in the neighborhood. They all had been involved in school, sports, parties, hanging out, and everything else kids do. But recently, he was confronted with a dilemma. During this past year in school, he had begun to experience the calling. Father Coppola, his religion teacher at Bishop Simmons, had spoken to him a number of times about the vocation to the priesthood. He was very helpful and certainly not pushing Skip in this direction, but he assured him if the calling were true, he would know. The more he searched within himself, the more Skip realized the certainty of his future. He thought of these guys as brothers and wanted to be included in everything they did. Spending this week with them was so important to him because it would be his last chance. He knew after graduating this year from high school he would choose to enter the Seminary.

He was always something of a loner. Wandering around Ocean Heights was okay. He wasn't interested in meeting girls, but wanted to experience the multitude of people and personalities coming together in this seaside resort. His travels had proven beneficial in helping him to understand the vast assortment of individuals and the families he would have to deal with someday. This trip had given him the time to contemplate if his decision to become a priest was real. He knew his choice was right.

The screeching tires caught him off guard. Twisting around, Skip saw the red Mustang convertible skid toward the curb. Two boys jumped out of the car and quickly pounced on him before he realized what was happening. Locked in the grasps of the larger boys, Skip was roughly thrown in the back seat of the Mustang landing on top of a prone figure. Instantly, he recognized the tousled, bruised face of Spider. One of Spider's eyes was beginning to shut from an ugly welt underneath and blood trickled from both sides of his nose.

"Sorry, man," he whimpered in pain. "I tried not to say anything, but they wouldn't stop punching me."

"Spider, are you okay?" shouted Skip. His question was met with a wicked punch to the side of his head.

"Shut up, you little queer!" Jason screamed at him as he slammed the car into gear and tore into the driving lane.

A Lasting Summer

"I told you, this Spider, local homo would know where to find this holy-roller." Evan laughed in vicious contempt. "I never thought we would catch his sorry ass so fast. Nailed the sucker coming out of church."

Skip's brain swam in a thick vortex of semi-consciousness. The blow to his head had caught him completely off guard and its effects were preventing him from helping Spider or himself. He was questioning the reason for this attack on both of them. He quickly recognized Jason and knew something bad was going to happen.

Jason slammed his foot to the gas pedal weaving in and out of traffic. He was in an adrenalin rush after the attack on the two boys and what he was planning for them. He had spent the night searching all along the boardwalk for this group of guys hanging around Tori and her friends, but never found any of them. Lucky for him, Mona called late last night to tell him she knew where Tori and her friends had gone. He never thought about them heading to Rocky Point. This time he was out foxed, and he was pissed. Today he would even the score with the whole lousy bunch.

"Hey, we pulled this part off pretty easily," Evan cackled.

"Yeah, we got two of these losers, but I want them all." Jason blasted through a red light barely missing two old people crossing the street. "Pay back is a bitch and I'm collecting the bill!"

An hour later, Drew and Pat O'Donnell were walking into Jan's Dare to Wear Beach Shop. Pat had grown up with Andy and he knew him better than anyone. After last night, he knew his friend was in turmoil. He convinced Andy to go and talk to Tori about whatever was bothering him so much. Red even offered his support by accompanying him to the shop. Drew gave in with little argument to his friend's advice.

"Hi, guys. Hope we didn't keep you up too late last night." Kelli pleasantly greeted their unexpected arrival.

"Do you work here, too?" asked Red.

"No, I just hang around to give my best friend some company."

Tori came out of the back storeroom. Her eyes immediately met Drew's.

"Hi, Andy. I was hoping you would come in."

"I wasn't sure if you would be here this early."

Kelli led Pat toward the front of the store to give her friend some privacy.

"I hope you don't have anything bad to tell me," Tori uneasily spoke.

"I have so much to tell you," whispered Drew, "and so much to explain about . . ."

The door slammed inward.

"We have to help Spider!" Cody screamed hysterically. "Tori, Andy, we have to get out there to help them!"

"Cody, what's happened?" Kelli grabbed him by the shoulders trying to calm him down and control her own panic.

"Spider called me from a pay phone out near Memorial Bridge. Jason and his goon grabbed him this morning when he was delivering his papers to the boardwalk stands. They wanted to know where he could find you guys, especially Andy."

Cody was shaking in fright.

"Spider wouldn't say a thing, so they started punching him out. He finally told them about Skip."

"What about, Skip?" Drew fired out.

"He goes to church every morning. Spider spotted him a few days ago coming out of St. Anne's over on 26th Street. Since then, he sees him every day. Skip made him promise not to tell anyone."

"I knew he was having a problem," Red quickly added.

"Jason grabbed Skip on his way back from church. He was taking both of them over to Roosevelt Point and waiting to get Andy there for a fight."

"Come on, let's get the rest of the guys," Red shouted.

"No, no we don't have time," Cody replied in a terrified voice. "Spider got away, but he heard them talking about using Skip as bait."

"I have my car around the corner," Kelli burst out. "Tori stay by the phone."

Tori wrapped her arms around him shaking in fear. "Andy, please don't go. Jason is a vengeful, sadistic person who won't stop at hurting others. He's going to try to get you."

"I have to help my friend," Drew replied without any hesitation as he held her tightly.

Seconds later, Cody, Red, Kelli and Drew sprinted out the door, hoping they wouldn't be too late to rescue their friend.

Roosevelt Point was a narrow spit of sand dunes and beach twisting out from the shipping terminal of Port Republic. It was nothing more than another isolated stretch of Maryland coastline bordering the busy commercial harbor routes. It lay about three miles from Ocean Heights, but this distance was measured in a straight line directly across the water, so traveling by road increased it almost to ten miles. The only visitors it attracted were the occasional surf fishermen or beach walkers searching for rare shells.

Kelli stomped her foot to the gas pedal. The tiny four-cylinder engine whined in protest with the weight of its passengers. Fortunately, the Memorial Bridge traffic was light considering it was early morning and most of the cars they passed were heading toward Ocean Heights. Kelli spun the VW convertible off the main highway as they coasted down the last bridge span. A small two-lane road led from the inter-coastal turnpike toward the ocean with a weathered, rusted sign indicating Roosevelt Point.

They hadn't traveled a mile when a fiery red Mustang tore by them in the opposite direction. Drew immediately recognized Jason perched behind the wheel with his accomplice kneeling on the passenger seat holding both hands up giving them the finger.

"Hey, something is wrong," Red announced, but everyone else in the car was already thinking likewise. "Skip wasn't with them, and they didn't wait around to fight us."

Cody excitedly pointed in the direction of a boarded up, closed down gas station. A pay phone booth was tucked alongside hardly visible from the road. A small figure sat on the floor weakly waving his arm. Kelli slammed the brakes skidding across the gravel parking lot.

"Spider, are you okay!" Cody was shouting as he leaped over the side of the VW Bug. In a moment, he was at his friend's side.

"I'm so sorry," Spider painfully spoke. His eyes were red and swollen. "I didn't want to tell them, but they kept slapping me in the face and head, then punching me in the stomach." He clutched his side in pain.

"Don't worry, man, it wasn't your fault," said Cody reassuringly. "You did your best."

"Spider, where's Skip?" asked Red hurriedly as they huddled around him.

A Lasting Summer

"I think they left him at the Point, but I don't know why they left before you got here."

They helped the bruised Spider into the VW's front seat as gingerly as possible. Drew, Cody, and Red sat on the boot cover of the convertible. Two miles further the road came to an end at a narrow draw squeezed between ridged sand dunes. Scampering up the loose packed dunes, they squinted in the blaring sunlight looking out toward the ocean. The thin strip of beach was completely deserted with the exception of driftwood, pieces of timber, and a couple of old damaged rowboats.

"They must have come from some ship that went down in a storm," Cody pointed toward the useless, battered skiffs.

"There's something out there!" Drew shouted. His eyes had caught the irregular pattern of an object floating on the surface about a half-mile from the shore.

"It's one of the boats," said Cody, "and it looks like someone is in it."

Red shouted, "It's Skip!"

Realizing what he had seen, Drew began to make out the outline of Skip, but something was wrong with him. Lying almost on the bottom of the small boat, his head was propped up so he could barely see over the sides, but he wasn't moving.

"I think he's tied up or something," Drew said, "because he's not moving around or trying to get out."

"Oh, my God!" Kelli screamed in panic. "He's drifting out to the main channel where the riptides and currents will carry him out to the shipping lanes. The freighters will never see him in that little boat."

Almost in unison, they lifted their gaze outward. What they hoped not to see was suddenly there. On the horizon, a gigantic ocean-going freighter was making course toward them. Some quick mental calculations put Skip in the direct path of the floating monster.

"Kelli, take us back to the phone booth," Cody started sprinting down the dune. "We have to call the Coast Guard to get a rescue ship out to him."

"We won't make it in time," she shouted to him.

"If I only knew how to swim," Pat dejectedly spoke.

Drew quickly pondered the crisis. He was in a life and death situation with someone he hadn't even known before this week. Was this really happening, or was it part of his dream? He didn't know the answer, but he did realize something. He never competed in school on any sport team because he was so unsure of himself. Too frightened to compete and too shy to be around others, he chose not to participate. Drew knew he was a strong swimmer. He had spent so many summers in his backyard pool just swimming laps to occupy his lonely days. Unknowingly, he also possessed the prowess and the abilities of an exceptional athlete. He was Skip's only hope.

"I'll get him," Drew quietly spoke out as he shed his sneakers and shirt.

"No, Andy, no! Kelli pleaded. "You'll never be able to reach him and survive the rip currents."

It really didn't matter what she said. Drew had made up his mind. A short run from the dunes and he was plunging headfirst into the crashing waves. Drew settled into a smooth, powerful stroke as the sandy bottom fell away from underneath him. Using the contrasting color of the water, he angled toward the outgoing rip current. Less than a minute later, Drew felt as if he were on a high-speed conveyor belt made of water. He sensed his floating body being dragged out toward open water. As best as he could

A Lasting Summer

tell, Skip was still a good five hundred yards ahead of him, but in the background he spotted the freighter looming toward them.

Survival procedures describe the best method of escaping from the throes of a rip tide—swim perpendicular to the out-rushing river of sediment-laden water. Drew was chewing up yards of ocean with his untiring, crashing strokes, but he was swimming with the current. He knew the risks. Every yard he swam put him further from shore and safety. Along with this, the churning ocean freighter grew closer. It didn't really matter. His friend's life was driving him on.

Ten minutes later, Drew started to feel the burn in his arms and legs. Fatigue was creeping into his muscles and his breathing was becoming labored. The rip current was beginning to lose momentum, but so was he. Drew had closed the distance to less than two hundred yards, yet his tired body couldn't gain any ground. A wave pushed him upward. From this height he saw the inevitable. The little boat was in the direct path of the onrushing ship. He gathered up every bit of strength left and pounded into the waves.

Skip felt the vibrations of the ship's bow cutting through the waves and its props churning thousands of gallons seawater. The deep metallic rumble of powerful engines filled the air. His little skiff was leaking so badly, he hardly thought he would have made it this far. He had no idea why Jason did this to him. Maybe he only intended to scare him at first by tying him up in this beat-up lifeboat and letting him drift around, but the out-rushing river had unexpectedly propelled him toward open water. Skip was terrified by the possibility the little boat would sink or capsize. With his hands and feet tied together, he wouldn't be able to swim or keep himself afloat. Praying as hard as he could, the derelict skiff held together, but this new threat was overwhelming. As an occasional wave spun the lifeboat around, Skip kept catching intermittent views of the approaching vessel. Without even seeing, he sensed the proximity of the onrushing monster.

The surging wave pushed ahead by the mass and speed of the freighter brushed the lifeboat off to the side like a wind blown leaf. The tiny boat tossed and twisted in the enveloping, cascading waves. Hanging on for dear life, the lifeboat performed exactly as its designers had wanted. The freighter's rusting flank rushed by causing the skiff to bob and spin like a cork. Fighting to stay afloat, the combined weight of the onboard water and its weakened framework proved to be too much for the little lifeboat. A tidal wave of foaming, bubbling salt water created by the wash from the freighter's massive twin propellers exploded the derelict into a pile of unrecognizable debris.

Skip was tossed out of the boat as the final wave hit. Luckily, the ropes around his hands were torn away with the force, but his feet remained tightly bound. He started to tread water with his arms trying desperately to keep his head up.

The freighter moved on, unaware of its collision with the unseen craft and its passenger. The effort to remain afloat was draining every ounce of Skip's energy. He knew he had only seconds left before the muscles in his arms and shoulder would cramp and he would slip beneath the surface. There was no panic in his efforts only a peaceful acceptance of his predicament. Skip's faith was giving him the strength. Slowly, he slipped under the surface of the water as a murky veil gently drifted across his eyes.

A Lasting Summer

"Not yet, damn it!" Drew thought.

He dove downward grasping the inert form by his shirt. With a superhuman effort, Drew dragged Skip upward, away from the beckoning darkness and certain oblivion.

Struggling to keep the both of them afloat, Drew tossed his free arm over a piece of drifting wood from the shattered skiff. Seconds later, Skip jerked in a spasm of retching coughs, expelling water from his lungs. His eyes were glassy, but he was starting to recognize Drew.

"Andy, where did you come from?" Confusion mixed with shock reflected Skip's expression.

"I didn't take a boat out here, if that's what you're asking," Drew smiled. "I just decided it was a nice morning for a swim in the ocean."

"Thanks. You saved my life."

"You would have done the same for me."

Skip put his free arm around Drew's shoulder embracing him the best way he could in the situation they were in.

"We still have to make it back to shore before another one of these ocean dinosaurs comes rolling through again," said Drew.

They had been carried almost a mile off shore. Drew realized he couldn't swim the entire length back with Skip. His muscles still burned from his desperate sprint to reach Skip just when the freighter arrived. Hopefully, Kelli had contacted the Coast Guard, but how long would it take to reach them.

Twenty minutes passed. Drew was fighting to ignore the pain and fatigue. Fortunately, the swell on the ocean surface was a slight two-foot roll, so he didn't have to battle waves. He had tried to untie Skip's legs, but it was impossible without a knife. Drew focused inward and just concentrated on staying afloat.

Suddenly, Drew heard the faint ringing of a bell. Skip perked up, so he knew his friend must have also heard something.

"Is it a boat?" asked Skip.

"I don't think so," Drew answered.

The ringing kept getting louder. Drew tried to look in the direction it was coming from. There, he spotted a slender pole sticking upward. A few more yards and the red bobbing form of a channel marker came into full view.

"Skip, it's some kind of buoy. Some big metal cylinder floating around."

"Yeah, I think those are the markers the Coast Guard sets up."

Slowly, Drew treaded water hanging on to the wood and dragging Skip along. They made their way toward the buoy. Before long Drew was reaching for a thin metal railing circling the base of the marker. Skip followed his lead. For the moment, they relaxed trying to regain their strength.

"Were you scared out there?" Drew asked in between the rhythmic chimes from the marker's bell.

Skip nodded, "I was, but I had faith to accept whatever was asked of me."

"I'm not sure what you mean."

"I guess many people don't. Something happens at a point in your life and all of the sudden things become clearer."

Drew shrugged his shoulders confused by the words. "If you say so."

"Why did you risk your life for me?" Skip asked.

Drew thought for a moment. He hadn't considered the danger to his own life only the predicament Skip was in.

"You're my friend."

A Lasting Summer

A loud, wailing shriek pierced the air. The hailing signal from the Coast Guard cutter was beckoning to the boys. The sleek vessel knifed toward them. Waves of agitated water sparkling with sunlight rolled off to either side of the speeding ship.

Drew and Skip were about to be rescued.

It had been a hectic morning lasting into an equally busy afternoon. The boys were picked up and brought back to the Coast Guard base at Port Republic. By the time they were both checked out and cleared by medics at the base infirmary, the rest of the guys had arrived. Kelli, Cody, Spider and Red were already there and somehow they had contacted their friends back in Ocean Heights.

Drew walked out the infirmary door and was besieged by the cheers of his friends. Tori rushed to him, wrapping her arms around his neck, dragging him forward and kissing him at the same time. Tears of happiness and relief flowed down her cheeks.

"Oh, my God, I'm so happy you're safe," Tori wept openly. "I can't believe Jason would do anything so malicious."

"Hey, stop crying," Drew chided trying to pick up her spirits. "It was nothing."

"It was the bravest thing someone I have known ever did."

"Thanks. It means a lot coming from you."

The celebration continued, but an undertone was running through the group. Retaliation toward Jason and his friends was being discussed.

"Hey, guys, don't be stupid," Kelli spoke out sternly. "Jason is not worth getting arrested for."

"Are you out of your flocking mind," Roach chirped up. "These preps need a lesson on how to treat people."

Kelli walked right up to him and got in his face. "The Coast Guard will contact the Ocean Heights police, so why don't you wait to see what happens next."

"Okay, okay, but we are leaving tomorrow, so I'm not waiting all night."

Tori squeezed Drew's hand tightly. Something was bothering her more than ever, but she couldn't talk about it, not here and not now.

Plans were made. The group would meet at the boardwalk pavilion by eight o'clock.

Saturday night on the boardwalk always collected a huge crowd of tourists and vacationers of all ages. Families with a range of children, older couples, single people, middle-aged mothers and fathers, and of course the ever-present scores of teenagers. For many it was their first night on the famous boardwalk of Ocean Heights, for others, it was a sad end to a fun week of sun, sand, water, and friends. Tonight was the finale for the boys from Columbus. What began as an unplanned week had unexpectedly transformed itself into a series of remarkable days, events, and some new friends.

The guys had gathered at the pavilion as planned. Despite Skip's insistence to forget what Jason had done to him, Roach, Howie, Jeff, and Reeger wanted to lash back at the arrogant preppies. One bad action was about to cause another to happen.

"He stays at the Harbor Point Hotel," mentioned Cody as the boys were trying to find the best way to quarter the treacherous Jason.

"Yeah, but he won't be there now," said Spider. His face still bore testimony to the savage harassment he had received earlier.

A Lasting Summer

"Let's cruise the boardwalk then," Roach fired out, "because you know he'll be somewhere around here."

"I'll start looking for his Mustang with Jeff and Reegs," Howie replied.

The group was breaking up into search parties when Kelli and Tori walked into the pavilion.

"Hey guys, the hunt is over," began Kelli. "Your boy won't be found in these parts anymore."

"What are you talking about?" someone spoke out.

"My dad's friend called and spoke to him about the incident," Tori quietly began. "He's a county sheriff and he received the report. The Coast Guard already filed charges against Jason and his friend Evan about a maritime law regarding reckless endangerment in coastal waters. They reported it to the Ocean Heights Police Department and Jason was arrested on a misdemeanor. His father bailed him out, but he is banned from Ocean Heights for the rest of the summer. He's on his way home to Boston right now."

A cheer and shouting broke out. Justice had been served, but almost at the expense of an innocent person. The plans were quickly changed to enjoy the rest of the evening together on the boardwalk.

Tori seemed subdued and pensive. Drew could detect her uneasiness.

"What's bothering you, Tori?"

"Something I think you wouldn't understand."

"Come on, let's walk toward the pier where we can be alone."

They found a bench in the shadows away from the glitz and glitter of Playland's lights. Music could gently be heard wafting out from a speaker tucked away in a forgotten spot. They sat quietly staring at the ocean as a ghostly blackness crept over it.

"I want to thank you for giving me the most wonderful summer of my life . . . It was so heavenly, you meant the world to me, and anyone could see that I was so in love."

The lyrics to the song drifted through the air. Tori softly cried. Drew paid closer attention to the words having such a profound effect on her.

"I never will forget that summer day we met, you were so shy and yet you stole my heart away . . . we strolled along the sand walking hand in hand, then you kissed me and I knew that I would love you my whole life through."

"Wonderful Summer." Tears fell from her eyes.

"And though it broke my heart that day we had to part, I'll always thank you for giving me the most wonderful summer of my life."

"It sure has been, and now we have to part, like I knew we would. How true," she whispered.

"Tori, it's not my fault. I can't help it if I live in Columbus."

"I realize that, but I also realize I'll never see you again."

"I promise to write to you, and, and," Drew was becoming just as upset and starting to lose his bearings.

She cut him short. "That will never happen."

"Why not?"

"Happiness never comes that easy. You've come into my life by surprise, but you mean so much to me. I know it's only been a short time, but I know how I feel. I hardly think you feel the same way."

"That's not true!" Drew was on his feet. "I never had anybody like you in my life. I just don't know what to say."

"I know you don't feel anything."

"Tori," Drew caught his breath, "I don't know how to tell you the truth."

A Lasting Summer

"What truth?"

Drew rallied his courage. "I am not really what you think I am."

Tori was more confused than ever.

"I am not from this time. My name is not Andy, but Drew. Somehow I took my father's place in his past."

Minutes later, Drew had told her about his encounter with the Captain under the pier, waking up in another time period, and meeting a bunch of guys who mistakenly took him to be their friend and his father, Andy Michaels. Tori leaped to her feet.

"Andy, that's the most ridiculous story I ever heard!" She responded in a fury. The tears had dried in the corners of her eyes. "If you don't ever want to see or hear from me again, why don't you just say it?"

"Tori, I love you!"

She burst into a deluge of tears. "Goodbye, Andy!"

Just as quickly, she sprinted toward the boardwalk. Drew froze in shock at what he had told her and how she had responded. He jumped off the bench trying to catch up with her. His effort proved useless, as she quickly disappeared into the hundreds of people walking the boardwalk.

Minutes passed as Drew desperately searched for Tori.

"Hey, sonny, lost something?"

The voice had a familiar ring to it. He spun around to see Francine stooped over a cane.

"Where did you come from?" he asked.

"I live here, dummy."

"Yeah, I sort of heard about you."

"Pretty famous am I?" she cooed. "I think you need some help."

"Yes, yes, I really do!"

"You might want to visit the Flower again."

"What are you talking about?" he shouted. "Everybody keeps talking about some flower and I don't know what they mean!"

Francine perked up. "Sometimes you can be pretty dense, boy. You've been around it the past two days."

"Oh my God!" Drew broke into a sprint weaving in and out of groups of people on the boardwalk. Five minutes later he was crashing through the doors of 'Fortunes from the Sea.'

"I know you're here!" he cried out in the empty room.

The rear curtain slowly parted. A red satin gown was adorned with scarves of contrasting colors and jewelry of every type and shape covered her hands, arms, and neck. The woman's beauty was exquisite and breathtaking. Jonne appeared quite differently than she had the past two days.

"Why did you deceive me?" Drew asked.

"I did not want to hurt you," Jonne began, "because I could not give you all the answers you were searching for. Some things you needed to learn on your own."

"But you could have helped me to get back home sooner."

"Is that what you really wanted?"

Drew froze. Everything that he had experienced rushed through his brain—Skip's rescue, all the locals, his father's friends, his father's life, but more so, Tori.

"I don't know anymore!" he shouted. "I don't know what I want."

Jonne placed her hand on his shoulders.

"Drew, look at me. You were given something that few people will have a chance to experience. You can never have your father back, but you were given a start to your new life. Never resent what happened, and those things that will not happen."

A Lasting Summer

"What do mean by that?" he said.

"I can't give you any more help," replied Jonne. "It's now time for you to meet again with the Captain."

"He's the person I've been trying to meet up again since this all happened."

"He's waiting for you down under the pier."

Drew needed something else.

"The Captain told me to search for the flower of the boardwalk for answers," he hesitated. "What do you have to do with all of this?"

"You found what you were looking for." Jonne smiled. "I am the Flower of the boardwalk."

Drew's eyes bulged.

"In Arabic, Wahra, pronounced Jonne, is the Rose. And, Zahrah in my language is the Flower."

All the pieces came together. The mysterious girl who had become his saving friend gave him a lasting hug. "Drew may your life be happy and at peace from this moment on."

Lost for words, Drew sprinted from the shop and broke into a run back toward the direction he had just come from. Trudging through the loose sand, he finally reached the gloomy shadows of the pier's pilings.

"Where are you?" Drew shouted. "Appear, why don't you? and give me some answers!"

"No need to holler," the voice came from somewhere behind the pilings.

A figure emerged from the dark shadows. The Captain appeared as he had done so a week ago.

"Hello, Drew. We meet again."

"Hello nothing," Drew replied sarcastically. "You seem to be calling all the shots."

The Captain smiled, "Sometimes I do."

"Why are all these things happening to me?" asked Drew.

"You had an opportunity to experience a part of your father's life just as he had at one time. You met his friends, enjoyed his week at the shore, and had some of his memorable encounters. But most importantly, you had a chance to learn about your father, something that was missing from your own life. All the things the Flower told you."

"How could this have happened?"

"Let's just say," the Captain went on, "your father was granted a special favor for his son that he left so unexpectedly, and so many years ago."

Drew shook his head in wonderment. "Was I dreaming about rescuing Skip this morning?"

"Quite to the contrary. Your actions were very brave and commendable. You placed the life of someone else before your own. You would have made an outstanding Lifesaver."

"Thanks Captain Reader, considering the stories I heard about you, I feel honored," Drew returned.

The Captain tipped his rain hat.

"Captain, I have one request," Drew hesitated. "I don't want to go back."

"I'm sorry, but you can't stay in Ocean Heights."

"No, no, I don't mean that," Drew spoke firmly. "I want to stay in 1965."

"Impossible. It is time for you to return."

"Please, I don't want to go back," Drew pleaded. "You don't understand. I've made friends here, something I never had before. More importantly, I met a girl . . ."

"I'm sorry you met Tori," the Captain cut him short. Slowly his features began fading into the shadows. "Even I cannot control destiny."

A Lasting Summer

"No, don't leave, Captain! You owe me this; you owe me a life with Tori!"

"Until another day, in another life, when we meet again." The Captain lifted his hand in departure, the same fashion as he did a week ago.

"I'm not letting you get away again!" Drew bellowed.

He broke into a wild dash toward the foreboding shadows. Instantly, Drew blindly crashed into an unseen, low hanging beam. As he drifted into the vortex of unconsciousness, he dreamt of Tori and wondered what he would wake up to this time.

CHAPTER THIRTEEN

Sunday, August 8, 2000

"I think there's something over here!"

The beams of light crisscrossed through the maze of pilings creating an almost surrealistic puzzle. More shouts and voices mixed together with the shadows of running figures lending to the confusion. The searchers found an inert form sprawled in the sand lying under one of the pier's lower cross-beams. When the flashlight beam touched the figure, an immediate reaction took place.

Drew's eyes fluttered open. A throbbing pain exploded from his forehead to the back of his skull. "Oh no," he thought, "not again."

A comforting voice told him to relax and not try to get up. Moments later, a swarm of rescuers circled Drew administering some preliminary first aid and preparing to put him on a stretcher.

"I'm okay, really I'm okay," said Drew. "This has happened to me before and I'll be fine in a few minutes."

A stern looking figure wearing the uniform of the Ocean Heights police force had other plans. "Listen son, you have a nasty bump on your head that needs to be checked out at the hospital. We need to contact your mother and let her know you've been found."

A Lasting Summer

"My mother? What's she doing here?"

The officer gave Drew a puzzled look. "I don't know if that bump on your head or the beer I smell on you is making you forget, but it was your mother who contacted us about you being missing the past four hours."

"What do you mean the past four hours? I just left Tori, and then I was talking to the Captain."

"Guys, get him up on the boardwalk and put him in the rescue truck. He definitely needs to be checked out by a doctor."

A million thoughts flashed through Drew's mind. Another untimely meeting with the Captain had resulted in him being knocked out again and waking up to another weird situation. These people were making it sound like his mother was here. Could it be? Was he back where it all began a week ago? A sickening feeling rushed through his head. What happened to all the guys—Red, Roach, Howie, Reegs, Jeff and Skip? What about his friends in Ocean Heights—Cody, Spider and Kelli? What about Jonne? His head pounded more intensely from what he feared the most. Where was Tori?

Drew slipped into a passive silence. He relived every minute of the week he had, or maybe didn't have. Could the collision with the beam and his unconsciousness have created this entire scenario in his mind? He fought the idea with all his strength. It couldn't be just a dream. There was so much there, so many feelings. How could the Captain be so cruel to him, giving him so much hope and happiness and now just taking everything back.

The doors to the rescue truck were flung open and immediately Drew spotted his mother standing there. She was very upset and it was obvious she had been crying.

"Drew, I'm so glad you're okay," Karen Freemont sobbed, not able to hold back her emotion. "I never want this to happen again. I was so worried about you."

"It's okay, Mom," Drew quietly said. "I should never taken off from Aunt Betty's."

Before anything else could be said, Drew was carted off to an examining room. As he moved through the corridor, he noticed the time on a wall clock—1:35. Could it be possible this whole experience had taken place in only a few hours? Once inside the examination room, he lifted himself so he was sitting on the table. He scanned the room, nervously hoping to find the proof he needed. On the far wall, the calendar read August, 2000.

It was a long night for everyone. Drew was checked over by an attending physician in the ambulatory center, and other than a nasty bump and a bit of a hang-over, he was declared clear of any serious head injuries. After he was discharged, his mother drove them back to his aunt's house. It was a quiet ride and equally so as his aunt embraced him when he walked in. Everyone was exhausted from the sleepless night and the mental ordeal from his disappearance. Slivers of light began to form in the eastern sky. Dawn wasn't far away; nevertheless, Aunt Betty insisted they all try to get some sleep. Conversation could wait.

It was a fitful, restless sleep for Drew. Images flashed in his mind. It was so real, he knew it, but there was nothing to prove it actually happened. How would he ever explain to his mother or aunt what went on his whole week in Ocean Heights in 1965? More so, how would he ever find his friends and Tori again?

Around noon, Drew roused himself from bed with the hope of finding some answers. He knew only his aunt might have some insight or knowledge of the events taking place

A Lasting Summer

in Ocean Heights over the years. The smell of food carried through the house as he made his way downstairs. At least he knew his aunt was up.

"Good morning, Aunt Betty."

She turned around. "Morning to you, Andrew. It's so nice to see you're up and about." The kitchen was empty other than his aunt.

"Your mother took your sister to the beach. Maggie was anxious to go swimming in the ocean."

Drew grimaced at the mention of swimming.

"It's not all my business," she began, "but your mother was very upset last night. She worries terribly about you. I know the problem you are having with your father being gone."

Drew nodded. "Aunt Betty, can you tell me anything about my father?"

"Well, as I have said, he was a wonderful, happy, caring boy. He would always think about his family and friends first. I think that's why people were so attracted to him."

'Did you ever meet any of his friends?"

"One summer when your father was just about your age, he came for a week's stay here at the shore. He brought a group of his friends from back home, but I never met any of them."

"Why not?"

She smiled. "That week I went to Phoenix with your uncle. I think your father planned it that way so he and his friends could be on their own. He told me later on they had a vacation none of them would ever forget."

"Yeah, I bet," laughed Drew. "Did he ever talk to you about any people he met from around here?"

"You mean teenagers, especially girls, don't you." She was every bit as coy as she was nice.

"Sort of that."

"I'll be right back."

His aunt returned with a large binder. It was in all kinds of disarray with pictures and papers hanging out in every direction.

"This is our photo album, but I haven't done much with it since your uncle passed away. I imagine we can find something in here."

They paged through countless pictures of family members, friends, and scenes taken around Ocean Heights. Drew recognized many of the locations, including Rocky Point and the north end park, but he didn't want to reveal his knowledge. He was enjoying his aunt's nostalgic accounts, but it wasn't helping him find the answer he needed. Many photos showed his incredible likeness to his father. Drew understood why his father's friends could easily have confused them. As he flipped the next page, he froze in paralyzing shock.

"What's wrong, Drew?" His aunt questioned as she saw the look on his face.

"This, this, . . . ," he could barely mouth the words.

"Oh yes," his aunt began, "that picture was taken the week your father was here with his friends. We were gone, of course, but a neighbor saved it and gave it to me when we retuned. Cute picture, don't you think?"

Drew stared at the yellowed newspaper. It was the picture he and Tori posed for on the beach.

"It was taken by a photographer from the Herald and they put it into one of their weekly editions. The Herald used to be our local newspaper, but unfortunately it went out of business a while back."

He continued staring at the picture. The caption simply read, "Two teenagers enjoying a day during this wonderful summer." Nothing more. As hard as he stared, he couldn't tell if it was his father or himself in that picture. He did know for certain, Tori was the girl.

"Who's the girl?" he weakly mumbled.

His aunt was worried about how her nephew was acting.

"Drew, is this picture of your father upsetting you?"

"No, but I have to know who she is," he whispered.

"Well, if I remember, she was a lovely girl, lived on the next block over. She would always stop and talk to us on her way to the beach or her job. Her father was in the Navy if I'm not mistaken."

Drew sucked in his breath. "Does she still live around here?"

"No, unfortunately her father was transferred out west somewhere. They moved after Christmas the year that picture was taken."

All hope drained from Drew. Any chance of proving his mysterious week actually happened was fading, but more so, his hope of ever finding Tori again was also fading.

"Aunt Betty, would you mind if I keep this picture?"

"I would love you to have it," she said removing the picture.

Drew continued staring at the two figures. One of them he couldn't identify, and the other was lost forever.

After a late dinner, Drew asked his mother to walk with him. They made their way toward the boardwalk, a path he was very familiar. The sun was melting down the horizon leaving a trail of running colors. The ocean barely stirred as a soft breeze caressed its surface. The boardwalk was alive, but the unusually small crowd appeared subdued and quiet; a perfect evening for a talk and finding some answers.

His mother hadn't brought up the incident from the night before. He knew she was still hurting from the emotional strain and worry that something terrible had happened to him. Drew felt terrible not only for last night, but for the way he acted the past few years.

"I'm sorry for what I did last night, Mom, and what I put you through," said Drew as sincerely as he ever had.

Karen was taken back by her son's apology, but more so by his warmth.

"We all make mistakes at some points in our life," she replied softly.

"Yeah, I guess so, but it's not right to blame everyone else for them," Drew mentioned. "I think I've been doing it for too long."

His mother was amazed at what she was hearing. What did the accident do to her son? It was a long, long time since he had acted this civil with her.

They headed in the direction of the closed-down Playland. The crowd was thinning out even more near the old-end of the boardwalk. Drew passed food stands and shops different from yesterday, or more correctly, from thirty-five years ago. His stomach tightened as he approached the next store. Disappointed, he stared at what used to be Jan's Dare to Wear Beach Shop was now Sammy's Tattoo and Body Piercing Emporium. A little further down, Madam Zahrah's shop was a deserted parking lot.

"Mom, did you know any of Dad's friends?" he asked as they continued down the boardwalk.

"Sure. Friends he worked with, some from where we used to live, a couple from medical school. Is that what you mean?'

A Lasting Summer

"Well, I sort of want to know if you knew any of his friends from when he was growing up; anyone from his old neighborhood or high school."

She thought for a moment. "Not really. I grew up in Cleveland, so I didn't meet your father until after we were both out of college. However, he told me plenty of stories about a group of guys he grew up with who were absolutely crazy. They came from the same neighborhood and went to high school together. I don't know how they avoided not going to jail together."

They both laughed, but Drew knew it was totally correct.

"I wish I could remember their names," she continued, "but they were so unusual that I've forgotten them."

Drew wanted to shout out the names of the guys, but how could he ever explain how he knew them. His mother would be rushing him back to the hospital to get his head checked again.

They eventually reached Reader's Pier. Standing next to each other, Drew and his mother were mesmerized by the spectacular sunset.

"Mom, I don't know how to tell you this, but something happened to me last night when I was out alone on the pier." Drew paused building up his courage. "For the very first time in my life I finally felt a connection to Dad."

His mother started to cry.

"I was just so mad, never having a chance to grow up with him around, and not even knowing what he was like. Last night I think I began to understand. Just being here like he was when he was my age did something to me."

Karen wrapped her arms around her son. She had waited a lifetime to hear these words from him.

Drew's eyes began to well up. "I know why he stopped that night to help those people. He never would have had it any other way, even though it cost him his life. I only hope I can be like him someday."

"Drew, he loved you so much, and would be so proud of you today," his mother's voice was breaking apart with sobs.

"I will be different, I promise." Drew held his mother like he did when he was ten years old. "Mom, I just wanted you to know, I love you."

In a deserted alleyway, a hunched-over figure peered around the corner of the building she was hiding behind. Francine glanced at the mother and her son embracing. She smiled as a stunning girl with long black hair and dressed in a red satin gown looked over her shoulder.

"There's always something magical about the shore," she quietly spoke, "something that was always in your heart from the beginning."

The Flower blinked the tears from her eyes. "Sometimes one just needs the love of his friends to find it."

EPILOGUE

Sunday, August 14, 2012

The morning sun was slowly drying up the remnants of last night's thunderstorm. A cold front had pushed through the area bringing welcomed rain and a respite from the current heat wave. The air was clean and fresh, an invitation to enjoy the pleasant outdoor temperatures. People were all about strolling, jogging, sightseeing, and roaming through the concourse of sidewalks and tree-lined streets. The sights available were endless, especially if this was your first time in Washington, D.C.

The lone figure wandered with no apparent destination. Monuments, parks, and museums were all within walking distance. It was a just a matter of what appealed to one's interests. Past the White House, the Washington Monument, a walk through the Korean War Memorial and World War II Memorials, and a jaunt up the steps of the Lincoln memorial. The history of the nation was coming alive. Even though it might appear the figure was randomly choosing his locations, he had a particular destination in mind. The sidewalk meandered into the park, leading him to one of the most well known sights in America. The bronze figures were discolored with years of weathering, but their faces remained defined and poised. The three soldiers were cast in somber pain, suffering, and discouragement for the rest of eternity. The Vietnam War Memorial was testimony to the many lives sacrificed and the tragic times of another era.

For so many years he had hoped to visit this cherished monument. The Vietnam Wall was one of the foremost sights to see in Washington, but he also had a personal interest. An older, mature-looking Drew followed the walkway. Approaching the Wall, he immediately felt its enveloping effects. Absolute stillness blended with a soul reaching sorrow quietly emanated from the cold, black granite. He stood for a moment gripped in its power. Drawn by a sense of respect to the fallen, Drew trudged forward. Sadness and despair filled his heart, but a fear of what he might find could not escape his thoughts.

As the years of involvement in the war increased, so did the number of American casualties. The Wall rose higher in proportion to the inscribed names. Drew recited prayers in his head to the many fallen, wishing they had another chance at a life they never finished. He slowly moved along, passing others in a similar state of remorse. Fear grew as he approached the panels marking the late sixties. His friends from Ocean Heights, or were they from his dreams, would have been of age to be in Vietnam and perhaps victims of the conflict. He scanned the names. None of the names matched with his father's friends. The decade of the sixties faded away and once into 1971, he breathed a sigh of relief. His guard was down as his eyes randomly locked onto a single name. Terror and shock rippled through his body.

"It can't be," Drew whispered in a wavering voice. "No, it's not possible. Oh, my God, no!"

Twelve years had passed, but the name would be with him forever. He was staring through tear-filled eyes at the inscription, *Victoria Randall*. It couldn't be. It couldn't be her name on the wall of the Vietnam deceased. Victoria, shortened to Tori.

Drew staggered from the memorial, wobbling on the path, away from the unbelievable. At the end of the walk, another statue was tucked in a small clearing surrounded by benches. He collapsed into the closest one. In front of him was the Vietnam Women's Memorial dedicated to the women who served and died in the war. Three female nurses posed in their duties of aiding and comforting the wounded and dying of Vietnam. The same dream Tori had: to be a Navy nurse.

He sat in an envelope of silence, removed from everything around him. There wasn't a time that passed when he didn't think about Tori and the week at Ocean Heights. His whole life turned around from that moment. His last year in high school was completely different from all three before. Drew competed on the school's swim team, joined clubs and organizations, and made friends. Four years later, he graduated from Ohio State, and in another four years he was presented a degree from Johns Hopkins Medical School. He was now Doctor Andrew Michaels, MD. Maybe it was inevitable. His mother said it was a miracle, not that he became a doctor, but what had happened to him at the shore that summer. Maggie, his step-father David, and his mother were so proud and happy. Somehow, Drew knew his father felt the same way.

Tori was special to him. He never did find out anything about her afterwards that summer. While in college and medical school, he didn't have the time to get back to the shore. Aunt Betty had sold her house in Ocean Heights and moved to Phoenix. As much as he tried to believe it, he was never really sure his experience with his father's friends had ever happened. Maybe Tori was nothing but a dream or a figment of his imagination. Yet now, her name was engraved on a cold, black tablet of death. He stared at the figures in the statue—brave women serving their country, and for a few, making the ultimate sacrifice.

Drew was in Washington for a medical conference beginning tomorrow. He never expected his morning sightseeing would end up this way. Tears ran down his cheeks.

"Sir, can I help you in anyway?"

He glanced up. An older man dressed in the uniform of a park ranger was standing over him.

"I'm not sure," Drew replied in a broken voice. "My friend is on . . ."

He couldn't say the words to accept what he had seen.

"I am sorry for what you are going through," said the ranger. "Many others have had similar reactions when they recognize a name from the Wall."

Drew, quivering, asked for help. "Is there anyway I can find out more about this person?"

"Possibly, if there were any mementos or letters placed near the name. Every night we gather up all the items left here and take them to the Museum and Resource Center. The staff over there catalogues them and places them on display near to the panel section of the Wall."

"Thank you."

The ranger put a supporting hand on Drew's shoulder. He gave him a pamphlet that contained directions to the Museum. "I hope you find something there that might bring some comfort to you."

Drew weakly smiled.

Walking to the Resource Center, Drew reflected on his experience in Ocean Heights. Somehow his attitude toward his father had changed and with it, his whole life. Still, he could never figure out how his encounter with his father's friends had been possible. And of course, his feelings for Tori—was anything real? He needed some proof he was actually there.

The Park Service employee directed him to the section where artifacts were on display from the 1971 panel. His heart ached as he passed countless articles left in remembrance. Letters, tattered pictures, postcards, cloth insignias, medals, boots, lighters, bottles of hot sauce and beer, rosary beads, crucifixes, Star of David, unit flags, POW/MIA bracelets, different parts of uniforms, can openers, and rubbings taken from names on the Wall were all there—the memorabilia of a terrible page of American history.

It struck him with the force of a tidal wave. He prayed not to find something, yet he hoped for an explanation. In the display case of the 1971 collected items, a glass jar held a layer of sand with a photo perched on top. The yellowed picture was of two teenaged girls hugging each other on a beach with the ocean in the background. He recognized Tori and Kelli. Alongside, a clear laminated folder held two newspaper clippings. Drew saw the same one he had cherished all these years—Tori and him, or his father, on the beach taken the first day they met. The other was a clipping from the Ocean Heights Herald.

> Former resident, 1st Lieutenant Victoria Randall was killed in action on August 14, 1971 in the province of Chu Lai, Vietnam. Lt. Randall, a Navy nurse, was killed during a rescue mission under hostile enemy fire. For her valor, she was awarded the Navy Cross, posthumously.

Drew smiled sadly. He knew Tori would never have performed any differently.

"You would have made a great Surfwoman in the Life-Saver Service."

Tears fell freely from his eyes. She had been dead forty-one years to the day.

A handwritten note sat near the bottle of sand. Drew bent over so he could read the writing. He realized the message was from Kelli.

> *"Tori, you will always be my best friend. For the good times and fun we had together in Ocean Heights. For that special and wonderful summer when you met your first love, Drew. I love you sister, Kelli."*

Drew's mind fled to another time, another place when he walked on the beach holding Tori's hand. His father was Andy to everyone, but he was Drew. He only mentioned it once, but Tori had remembered. He was there, and she was real.

"Thank you, Tori, for saving my life. I'll never forget, and I will always love you."